F
H43   Herrick, William.
            That's life.

THAT'S LIFE

ALSO BY WILLIAM HERRICK

The Itinerant (1967)
Strayhorn, a Corrupt Among Mortals (1968)
Hermanos! (1969)
The Last to Die (1971)
Golcz (1976)
Shadows and Wolves (1980)
Love and Terror (1981)
Kill Memory (1983)

William Herrick

THAT'S LIFE

a fiction

A NEW DIRECTIONS BOOK

Manufactured in the United States of America
First published clothbound and as New Directions Paperbook 596
in 1985
Published simultaneously in Canada by Penguin Books Canada
Limited

Library of Congress Cataloging in Publication Data
Herrick, William, 1915–
   That's life.
   (A New Directions Book)
   I. Title.
PS3558.E75T44 1985 813'.54   84-27378
ISBN 0-8112-0946-6
ISBN 0-8112-0947-4 (pbk.)

New Directions Books are published for James Laughlin
by New Directions Publishing Corporation,
80 Eighth Avenue, New York 10011

To Griselda and Peggy

CONTENTS

The Bindlestiff	1
Nina—1	83
Osso Buco at the Gran Ticino	89
Nina—2	107
To Ma, with Love	111
Nina—3	155
Life—How Much Does It Cost?	161
Nina—4	191
Round and Round	195
Nina—5	217
The Devil with It	223

THE BINDLESTIFF

You said to put my story on tape the first chance I got, so here it is. I had a little accident and I'm flat on my back. Don't worry about it, my ass may be in a sling but I'm not ready for the pine boards. I love the world too much, its round belly pregnant with hope—yeah, hope, Max, stop bawling!—because to despair is to die, and paradise is to be neither dead nor alive.

I left paradise for the real world when I was fourteen. No, not the night Cleo Gordon and I screwed for the first time. (That was still paradise. Candy apples and Charlotte Russes. Sports and games. Hugs and kisses.) I was only thirteen then. They say the earlier you start, the longer you go. I hope it's true, though I have to admit that now I'm in my mid-sixties it takes a good deal longer to get the old thing fired up. But once it is, watch out, call the fire engines. (Look, you said for me to be myself, tell it the way I always am, so don't think I'm boasting or anything like that.)

Odd thing about the world, though—it gives you the old one-two, kicks your teeth in, doesn't go away. It picks you off the floor, dusts your pants off, pats you on the head, tickles your ribs, smiles when you laugh, then if you let your guard down, think you're back in paradise, whack! the old one-two again. Live or die—make up your goddamned mind, kid.

I remember my last night in paradise as if it was the night before last.

1931. Indian summer. The family is in the living room of our railroad flat. Outside the windows, the towers of the Williamsburg Bridge can be seen lit up, and if you listen for it, you can hear the subway trains rattling across. A mellow light shines through the silk lampshade with tassels and fringe. Pop and Mom sit on the over-stuffed sofa; Archie, my older brother, sits on the floor, little Davie and Sarah hanging onto his strong neck, and I, Maxie Miller, am lying on the worn rug with my head on my older sister Elsa's lap. (Nina, my youngest, is half Elsa, half Mimi, my wife's sister—tall, dark, and nifty.) Mom, her name was Miriam, is playing the mandolin and singing a Yiddish song. (I can still hear her voice right now, a warm alto. Like my Becky's, I wonder if that's why I fell in love with her, except my mom could talk up a storm when she got started and Becky's never been much of a talker, and lately even less than that.) Elsa's lap is hot and smells like warm bread just out of the bakery oven—you know, when they put the fresh bread on the shelves and you're walking by but you have to run in and take a good whiff with your eyes closed until they kick you out. I love Elsa and Mom and Archie and Pop and the little kids, though I hardly pay them any attention.

The scene's frozen in my memory. Pop's eyes are closed, his pockmarked hollow cheeks dead still. He's daydreaming of the old country, the muddy streets and little huts, and the goats stamping their hooves in the lean-tos against the rickety houses, and in his daydream Pop sees his mother and father and sixteen brothers and sisters, all of whom he left behind when he was eighteen and never saw again except for his sister Judith who lived in Trenton, New Jersey, with her family. Ma's singing softly. Only when she sang like that did her haggard, harassed face become round and beautiful like in the yellowed picture of her as a young woman that I keep in my bedroom drawer. She's singing a love song—two young lovers walk hand in hand along a winding river in the forest, they stop to eat berries right off the bush, they kiss passionately, and when they separate their faces are all stained with berry juice and they laugh. Archie hugs Davie and Sarah to himself and they are quiet for a change. I lie on the old rug with my head on Elsa's hot lap. Pop daydreams of the old country when he was a kid, and Mom strums the mandolin and sings in her sweet alto.

The next day, Eli Miller, my father, who was a roofer, slid off a steep slate roof he was working on down the block, and paradise was behind us. The boss locked us out, and we hit the bricks as they say. We were out in the world. The pain was real—no fucking dream.

My father Eli Miller was forty-two years old when he died. He worked hard to provide for his family. All the older people said he never lied and he never stole and he never raised his hand against another unless it was to protect his children. That was a tough neighborhood, plenty of hoods and young punks around. Everyone said Eli Miller lived and died a decent man. There's no reason for me to believe otherwise. That's the way I remember him, too. Though my mother, at one time or another over the years until she died, said he wasn't a saint, had had an awful temper like me.

So Eli Miller died and was buried, and Archie, Elsa and I, and probably Davie and Sarah, young as they were, saw the real world for the first time. I suppose my mother had already lived in it for quite a while.

We didn't know where the next buck was coming from. No more candy apples for me, and Charlotte Russes were for kings. It didn't mean I stopped playing punchball or screwing with Cleo Gordon or fighting in kid tournaments run by the Educational Alliance or, believe it or not, borrowing books from the public library. I loved reading books, everything from Horatio Alger to Zola, though I didn't much like school.

The Millers weren't the only family starving—the depression was sinking deeper and deeper. Archie got a part-time job after school (he was a freshman at City College and Mom said she would commit suicide if he quit), and Elsa, still in high school, worked for Lorraine the milliner on Second

Avenue, Saturdays, and we managed to eat no better and no worse than anyone else on the block. Pushcart crowds were smaller, the street was half dead, the breadlines were stretching longer, and it began to look like the whole world was on its way to the bone yard. You must have heard it off the other tapes you got for your study of the thirties, so I won't belabor it.

As I said, I was fighting in kid tournaments, and everybody said I was going to make it as a pro. Punchy Goldstein, smashed nose and lop-eared, the old time challenger to the world middle-weight crown, ran a gym down on Delancey Street, and I'd go down there and Punchy'd let me train, even took me into the ring himself and sparred with me, giving me instruction. Don't follow my eyes, yuh dope, jest my hands. My eyes can't hurt yuh, my hands can. . . . Keep yer wrists stiff like a ramrod otherwise y'll break 'em. . . . Balance, balance, always stay in balance. . . . The best advice a man—or woman—can ever get.

He saw me fight a couple of times, kayo my opponents, and he said, "'Attaboy, Maxie, you're gonna make it, you got the killer instinct . . . a fighter needs the killer in him if he wants to be champ." I loved the smell of the gym—the leather, the liniment, the sweat, the sound of a pug slamming the heavy bag, the ratatatting of the light bag, the wham of solid punches on some guy's gut.

Archie screamed at me—he hated fighting (though if he had to he could put a punk away with a roundhouse). He was a big bruising kid, dark, handsome, like my oldest son Eli named after my father; my mother, Elsa, they screamed, too. We don't want you to be a fighter, we want you to study, do your homework, read books, you have a brain, use it, we want you to be more than an animal, we don't have to be rich, just have enough to eat. Baloney, I'd yell back, I wanna make a good buck, school'll only get yuh on the breadline. Archie would shake me until my teeth rattled like castanets. Stop talking like a bum, he'd say. I'd break loose and run away.

I kept returning to the gym and Punchy taught me how to keep in perfect balance boring in or backing up, to use my elbows, my thumbs, my knees, every trick in the book, but most of all how to put every ounce of my body behind a punch so when I hit a guy he was hit for good. At fifteen, I could take almost any man my weight. I was built to be a middle-weight—the kind of frame that after it fills in when you're thirty or so becomes a good light heavy if you stay in trim. I was real good and that's because I loved it. I admit it. I did have the killer instinct. When I hit a guy solid and he went down on his ass, his eyes glazed, I felt like a million bucks.

But bad became worse, everyone in the house was becoming skinnier by the minute, Davie and Sarah were always crying they were hungry, and everytime I passed a restaurant and saw people eating meat I'd get an awful pain in my belly. Yeah, the dream, the myth, the legend, the paradise was gone. We were out in the world now—the Miller family was slowly starving to death. But that wasn't enough—once the sky opens up, the shit flops and the piss pours. Archie came down with pneumonia and some Jewish charity sent a couple bags of food. Too late. Archie died—a big, strong kid with a brain like a steel trap like my kid Peter, with the agility of a trapeze artist. He was so smart everybody said he was going to become a professor, a lawyer, a governor. Oh, yeah. He died. Now there was only my mother and four children. No welfare, no relief, nothing much from the government. At that time the world gave you nothing. Even the mice in the walls were starving to death.

I was fifteen and a half. I went to the gym. Spoke to Punchy.

"Get me a fight—we got nuthin' tuh eat."

"Can't . . . yer too young yet."

"I'm goin' on sixteen—I'm strong."

"Yer a big tough kid, Maxie, but yer too young. First yuh gotta go in the amachures—the Golden Gloves."

"We can't eat medals, Punchy. Elsa quit school and can't find a job. I can't neither. Mom can't. Every bite of food I take is right out of her mouth. The kids got black holes in their heads where their eyes are supposed to be. We'll lie, tell 'em I'm seventeen."

Punchy shook his head. "I gotta family, too . . . don't wanna lose my license."

"Fuck you," and I marched out half crying as Punchy stood there with a sad look on his smashed pug's face.

That night, Elsa, the little kids, and I sat at the kitchen table. Mom was frying a small piece of stale bread in a pan with some chicken fat she got from a neighbor. We were all quiet, gloomy—none of us smiled anymore. Mom sliced the fried bread and gave us each a piece. That was all there was. Elsa stared down at her bread, stared at Davie and Sarah, two pale little bags of bones. I eyed my piece, then looked at my mother. She looked thin, bitter, even mean.

"What about you, Mom?"

"Eat and shut up."

"No, Ma, you eat it." I shoved the plate away. Mom began to cry. Soon Elsa and the kids were crying, too.

I stood there—looked at my hands, big strong mitts. If I didn't get out of there I'd run amuck like that crazy Roumanian who'd killed his starving wife and kids with a butcher knife. Then I raised my head and stared at each of them as if to impress their images on my brain. The tears were rolling down their faces. That's all they'd had for a good year and a half. Tears and dying and hunger. I gazed around the kitchen. Dingy, poor. I was just another mouth to feed—what did they need me for?

I made up my mind, shrugged, and marched out.

Then ran and ran. Up Mulberry. Crosstown on Canal. Down Broadway to the Battery. Had two cents, mooched three more, took the ferry to Staten Island. Hiked, hitched to U.S. Route 1.

I was on the bum.

It's funny. You know I lost an eye fighting the fucking Nazis in Europe and the fake one I got acts like a silver screen inside my head and as soon as I think of the old days I get these images like a movie.

I'm on the road. A two-laner. Day . . . night . . . rain . . . snow. . . . A long, winding empty road meandering through endless acres of rotting grain fields. There was too much wheat on the market so everybody was starving to death. And there I am, Maxie Miller, sixteen years old, in rags, my broken shoes tied to my feet. I carry a strong hickory stick which I'd cut off a tree and trimmed with my knife. That stick and my two quick hands keep me alive.

I bummed the country. Stole, begged, chopped firewood for farmers' wives. I had those big mitts and a tough face. Some kid around the old block once broke my nose with a broomstick during a block fight. The way it healed is the way it is. I wasn't very pretty to start with, so what the hell difference did it make? Sometimes a farmer's wife would feed me and then let me put it in, and I'd cop a beat before her old man got back. As far as I could see they did it because their lives were so damned lonely, I because it came easy. Afterwards I thought of them as sluts. A piece of gash. That's what I had learned on the block, even at home. A woman did it with you, she was a whore; a man did it, he was a man. Angelo Ferrara tried to teach me different, but it took me a good long time to learn. Perhaps I'm just slow or perhaps it's what you learn as a kid that's hardest to un-learn. One thing is sure, as you get older unlearning is a lot harder than learning.

On the road I met hoboes, bindlestiffs, tramps, bums, old men, young kids my age, an occasional bimbo—that's a girl or woman on the run. To us it wasn't a derogatory word anymore than hobo was. It didn't mean whore, not to us anyway. A bimbo, bimmie, bim was just like us—moving, looking for something to eat, trying to keep warm. Sometimes a bimbo and I stayed together, scrounged, stole together, slept close to keep warm. If she felt like it, we did it—if not, we didn't. We were rough on the road, but we weren't animals, goddammit. Most of us anyway. Though I was halfway there when I met Angelo Ferrara. Much of the time I was alone. And that was the worst.

Whether it's a time of feast or of famine, it's always the same on the road for those who have run away. There's the fight to keep clean. You fight against giving up on it, saying the hell with it. There's always a river, a creek, a well, and if you want to you can stay clean enough. My clothes became worn, torn, ripped, my shoes broke in two, my socks worthless. Yet when I found a stream, I bathed myself, washed my ragged clothes. In summer, that is. Winters, well. . . . When I was with Ferrara, we were always clean. Years later it became sort of a fetish with me. I analyzed it. For years I thought I was filthy, rotten, ugly inside so I scrubbed my skin. When I was in the Army before the war, I was the neatest, cleanest man in the division, in the whole Army Corps. And the stall of my mule Edna—I was in horsedrawn artillery at Fort Meade (it sounds like a million years ago)—I kept it as tidy as a hospital room. I was *champeen* middleweight of the Eighth Army. Before a fight, in the locker room smelling of lysol and liniment, I'd shower, scrub every millimeter of my body, between my toes, my asshole, under my nails, every curlicue of my big ears. I'd rub myself apple red, put on my bleached white sweat socks, my metal jock, my boxing trunks, my starched robe, and say, "Keep yer hands off a me," to my seconds. My bell would ring and down the aisle between the screaming soldiers I'd dance to the ring, skip between the ropes to my corner. "Keep yer filthy hands to yourself," I'd repeat. No one was to touch me. Clean. Clean before I hit the sonuvabitch in the other corner. The bell. Kill the fuckin' kike! they'd yell. Murder the dirty wop bastard! Cut the Polack cocksucker to ribbons! I'd look at the guy in the opposite corner and say to myself, you lay your dirty gloves on me, you're a dead man. All of it would come out, every bit of it, all the murder in my head and heart, all that I'd saved up I let go on the man in the ring with me. I never even saw his face. He was merely someone to beat. And the more he hit me, the worse I'd beat him. Because I wanted to be clean, goddammit! CLEAN!

But that was after Angelo Ferrara, the numbness it left with me, and after I'd joined the Army because I wanted to make the world clean. Nuts, eh? Cleaned out lots of Nazis, too, believe me. One of the smartest things I ever did.

On the bum I was a tough, sullen kid. Strangely, I didn't fight too much and I could have fun and make people laugh when I wanted to. Shit, man, no matter how low on the totem pole you are, you still have to laugh otherwise you might as well be dead. Like that time in a garbage dump—I called every garbage dump Garbage City, though most everybody else called them Hoovervilles—outside Chicago. An old dude died in his sleep. Hunger? Heart? Just dead tired? Who knows. Before the city morgue wagon came I copped his old pearl-buttoned spats and derby hat. The spats on my feet, the derby at an angle on my head, I grabbed up my hickory stick and, in the center of the ring formed by my fellow citizens of Garbage City, I did a soft-shoe off to Buffalo like I'd seen in every vaudeville show they ever had in Loew's Delancey. They all clapped and I sang, "Snatched a little kiss in the mornin', kissed me a little snatch at night." That floored them. They really laughed. What were we supposed to do—cry because that old geezer had died? He wasn't the first, and certainly wouldn't be the last. When my mother was in her late years, she always used to say, "When I die, the night after my funeral, go see a comedy and laugh—you'll have plenty of time to cry in your old age."

Slept in barns, under culverts, in boxcars, in garbage dumps at the edge of big cities. Crisscrossed the country from Pittsburgh to San Francisco Bay, from Cheyenne to Santa Fe. Had my can whacked by every yard bull in every freight-yard from Joliet to Seattle and back again. There wasn't a hobo camp I didn't know plus any farmer's wife who was a soft touch. Only used my fists when I had to. Was saving it up. Once in a boxcar on a freight siding outside St. Paul—it was winter and it was so cold my piss froze before it reached the ground. What a rainbow! There were six of us in our rags with newspapers wrapped round our bellies, and we exchanged stories of our travels to keep awake so we wouldn't freeze to death in our sleep. When we finally did fall off it was belly to ass. The poor bastard behind me must have had a hot dream because I felt a nudge where I shouldn't have. I really rapped him one and was about to take him apart piece by piece when the others stopped me. A man has to stay clean on the road because if he doesn't there's only one direction he can go—downhill, and I was going that way faster than I now like to believe.

Late winter '34. Rough, tough, and wily, I straggled into the same Garbage City outside of Chicago where earlier I'd done a soft-shoe in spats, derby, and cane. Under my rags I had two spuds I'd swiped in the Windy City. My hair was wild on my head, and I still carried my hickory stick. If you latch on to a good weapon, hold onto it. In the valleys between the mountains of garbage, huddled shacks constructed of corrugated tin, old wood furniture, crates, and the like. Hoboes, bindlestiffs, bums, and tramps sat around small fires. Some smart guy once wrote, "Bums loafs and sits. Tramps loafs and walks. But a hobo moves and works and he's clean." He doesn't mention bindlestiffs. A bindlestiff's the same as a hobo, but with one main difference. A hobo's on the road by choice, that's the way he wants to live. Even in prosperous times, there are hobos on the move. But a bindlestiff was a guy who jumped the line because there was nothing to eat at home—it was either starve to death or bum the land. As far as I know biffs, as I called them, only appeared on the road during the depression. I was a biff. Oh, yes, another difference. Hobos despised those who bummed car rides—they either jumped freights or walked; a biff took what he could get, he had no snobby ideas about how he ought to get around. A bimbo's a female biff. A hobo's generally honest, he doesn't steal except as a last resort; a biff's not that particular, but only food, not money.

I shuffled into this Chicago Garbage City with these two spuds, and I spotted one group boiling a soup over their fire and headed straight for them, withdrawing my potatoes from under my laugh of a jacket as I approached them. That was to show my honorable intentions. There were five men and a bim. I didn't know her then, but did soon after. Her name was Tillie. She sat next to a guy named Ray. I didn't know him either. She was a young kid, perhaps seventeen or eighteen, thin, pretty if she hadn't been so damned dirty, wearing a skirt of rags, a torn sweater, an old cloche hat, filthy ripped sneakers. Around her shoulders hung a fur neckpiece, ratty, mostly naked of fur, the sort lifted from a garbage can. She was a quiet girl, hardly ever said a word, decent, sad. She had this nervous giggle—a scared bim, a waif, always cold. Ray was a skinny little man with wirelike muscles which coiled around his arms and legs. He had a long lean jaw and thin mean lips and his gray eyes stared at you hard. The hair on his head was wispy, the color of groats. He spoke rarely, and then only in curses. Beat me two to one.

I sifted through the ragged, tattered circle, showed them my potatoes with a dramatic gesture; they nodded, I took out my knife and sliced them into the soup pot, then shuffled over to Tillie—I like women more than men, I admit it, always did and always will (Becky, my wife, says I like them too blasted much). Tillie shoved her skinny rump over to make room and looked at me shyly behind her long eyelashes, a little scared, then giggled. Ray examined me from the other side of her with those hard eyes of his. I grinned, he nodded and picked up a half loaf of stale bread, broke off a small chunk, and passed it over Tillie's lap. She was his bim, I could see that immediately.

"Thanks, bud," I said, in a hurry to sink my canines into it. My bad luck that three hungry bums came along just then and stopped to stare at me as I chomped away. Suddenly one of them lunged for the piece of bread. I pulled it away in time, held it close to my chest. "Screw off, bum." His two buddies moved in close, and they sort of surrounded me.

To make it short, I had to decide whether to fight and chance losing the bread in the scuffle or just hold onto it and let them waste their energy on my shoulders and head. I made a quick decision and decided on the second. I hadn't had a piece of bread in days—so it came before vanity and dignity. I stood up, crouched over the bread clasped in my mitts, pulled my head in between my shoulders like a turtle as they slammed away. They didn't have much strength, they were too hungry. I'm not boasting if I say I could've taken the three of them in three seconds flat. They banged away at me and I danced around like a pro, a little grin on my puss to show I wasn't scared. Those sitting around the fire didn't pay us any attention, their eyes keen on the soup. Except for Ray and Tillie. She giggled nervously behind her thin hand; Ray stared hard at us. Just as I was beginning to lose my temper and screw the bread, Ray stood up, an empty milk bottle in his hand, and stepped towards our little dance.

"Leave the kid alone, yuh fuckin' cruds," he said, scowling like he meant it.

They stopped mauling me, looked at Ray a moment, and as they moved on him, he just raised that empty milk bottle over his head. When he stepped towards them, the bottle shining, collectively they thought better of it, turned tail, and ran.

"No hard feelin's," I yelled after them, laughing. For crissakes, they were hungrier than me.

Ray and I sat down again, flanking Tillie, and I thanked him for his help.

"This is my bim, Tillie," he said in a gravel voice. "I'm Ray."

"Maxie—Maxie Miller." We shook hands over her lap. She lowered her eyes.

We were friends now. That was all it took on the road.

Tillie pulled sunflower seeds from the pocket of her skirt and passed some to me. I put them in my pocket for dessert because the pot was now boiling and soon we were all standing at it to fill our tin cans. We sat around the fire soaking stale bread in the soup and eating, paying strict and honorable attention to our one and only meal that day.

When you're hungry, there's nothing else in the entire world. It's with you every waking and sleeping moment. It fills you up to bloating, it's yours alone. It sticks to your bones. It wraps itself around you—caresses you, kisses you, fucks with you. It's your lover—a nagging, scratching, impossible lover. You scream, let me alone! But no, it sucks you off, reams your asshole, cuddles up in your gut, nagging, mean, ripping, clutching. The soup tasted good. A bone stolen from a dog in a rich suburb. Parsnip tops from a garbage pail. Two spuds filched from a poor storekeeper in a slum. Stale bread given by a kind baker who stole it from his boss. A couple of carrots from a housewife. And a fistful of salt. A very good soup.

We hooked up—Tillie, Ray, and me. Hit the road together. A lonely road. Ray carried a bindle hanging from a long stick over his shoulder. I used my hickory stick like a dandy's cane. I still wore the spats—they kept my feet from freezing—but had long ago thrown away the derby. Ray always walked between Tillie and me. When she talked it was in a very low voice. "Let's stop, I have tuh take a leak." "Cripes, I'm cold." "Maxie, yuh want some sunflower seeds?" A shy smile, the soft cold touch of her fingers, that damned giggle. Even when they screwed at night in some hayloft or barn, she giggled. It would blow my sixteen year old mind.

I don't have to tell you every second of it, do I? Holy Moses, I have total recall and could keep you up for days. Just shots of us oughtta do.

At the backdoor of a farm house, begging food from a farmer's wife. A wind's blowing across the fields, the trees bare, stark against the horizon.

A long freight curves slowly out of a railroad yard. I jump a flat car as Tillie and Ray run alongside. I grab her reaching hands as Ray heaves on her tail. Then he jumps on.

We stand in a line at a soup kitchen in Detroit surrounded by hollow-cheeked, starving black and white men, women, and kids. A white guy's bullying a rickety brown boy. We— Negro and white—turn our eyes, all we're interested in is the steaming pots. On the wall hangs a picture of a smiling FDR. As long as guys my age remain alive he'll be The President.

A late winter snow. We stand at the periphery of a large crowd listening to a street corner agitator. He's surrounded by guarding workingmen. A riot wagon empties of cops, who come at the speaker and his guards with swinging clubs. A big fight—the workers giving as much as they're taking. The three of us duck out.

The snow's melting, the trees have tiny buds and swing gently in an oncoming spring breeze. Ray chops wood in a farmyard.

Tillie and I are lying in a field off a country road, waiting for Ray. She's got her eyes closed. Suddenly I stroke her shoulders—the first time—and she doesn't move away, just keeps her eyes closed. I continue to caress her shoulder gently, dying to put my hand on her small hard breasts. Stop abruptly and move away, shaking my head. Tillie giggles, snaps it off, opens her eyes, stares at me, her face sad. Hell, we've been as close as you can get, but the law—not the world's law, our own law—says no.

A flaming red and purple twilight. Three tiny figures amble over the hill of a two-laner that runs through large barren fields. There are no barns or houses in sight. We're between Bay City and Saginaw in Michigan and it looks like we're on the moon.

It's the three of us. Ray's shouldering his bindle, I'm twirling my hickory cane. Ray's speaking, Tillie on his far side's cracking and eating sunflower seeds, and I'm eying her from behind his back. Every once in a while we catch each other's eye. She's fielding sunflower seeds from her pocket, breaking them open with her tiny pointed teeth, sucking out the meat, and chewing. I tell myself, you're gonna have tuh jump the line soon.

Night approaches quickly. Ray points ahead to a large culvert running under the road.

Soon a small fire's burning inside the culvert. It's like a cave. Ray and Tillie sit together on one side, I alone on the other. She and I belong to each other as much as she and him. We've bummed, begged, swiped, and worked together, helped each other stay alive. I know her smell as well as he does. And she's mine as well as his. I can feel myself getting mad, bitter. A half-filled bottle of milk stands near him. I'm cutting a loaf of bread a farmer gave us for shovelling manure. I cut it into three equal portions and pass them theirs. We eat our bread and take turns on the milk bottle until it's empty. Ray keeps the bottle at his side. A bottle is his weapon, just as my hickory stick is mine. Sporadically, Tillie hums a song, snitches a look at me from under her long eyelashes, giggles softly and even more nervously than usual—she's no idiot, just a scared, lost girl on the bum. She worked, she mooched, she swiped as well as either Ray or me. By this time Ray and I hardly noticed her giggling any more than you notice your own breathing.

Outside the concrete culvert it's night. Freezing cold. On the same two-laner, Angelo Ferrara, a brawny bullheaded man of fifty-eight, is driving a flivver pickup truck, the back enclosed in a handmade wood body. Neat, shipshape. His worker's cap is pulled down over his ears. He's driving very fast, because that's the way he always drives. In my mind I can see him hunched over the wheel, obviously cold. He's whistling an aria from some opera, steam escaping from his nostrils.

In the culvert I'm half sleeping on my side of the fire, Ray and Tillie on theirs. We've had some food, the fire's warm, and they've had a fast fuck, goddamn them. I could hear every second of it—even the sharp slap slap as they pumped away. Now he's snoring, and I'm lying there with a hard-on like a burning horn between my legs. Suddenly my ears grow large. I can hear Tillie stir. I pretend I'm dead alseep; she's probably going out to take a piss. I hear her crawling on all fours. She's around the fire, and I hold my breath until she stops near me. Her light hand touches my shoulder. I still pretend I'm asleep. She shakes me a little harder. I sit up, wiping the pretended sleep from my eyes. Tillie's staring at me, the fire striping her face. We stare into each other's eyes. Hers are so damned sad. She's telling me with her eyes that she wants to give me something, a present, a little gift, but neither of us move. We have our own law and we have to live up to it. But she wants to be kind, and I want her more than anything else in the world. So I put my hand out and caress her smooth thin cheeks. Gentle, sweet, that's all. And she smiles at me, gentle and sweet, too, and so fucking sad—for me, she's being sad for me. And I'm so hungry for her, to hold her, to feel her close to me, to kiss her and I don't know what to do. Ray's snoring real heavy. She smiles sadly again, takes my head in her thin hands, and kisses my face with her eyelashes, and I can't hold myself back any longer, with a rush I take her in my arms, crush her to me, and her little body is so warm, hot, and it fits under mine like it belongs, and I pull her ragged skirt back over her belly and my horn is so hard and hot, too, and I want to put it into her, to love her and have her love me and she keeps kissing my face with her eyelashes and we begin to roll, to move up and down—and there it is—that nervous giggle of hers. It rolls around the curved walls of the culvert like crackling thunder. I tell you, I can hear it better now than all the artillery barrages I ever lived through.

I pulled away. Too late. Ray sat up, looked for Tillie at his side, saw she was gone, threw a terrified glance in my direction, cried out in pain. My God, I can still hear it and it rips my heart open. I roll off Tillie and she crawls away towards Ray. There is no time now for chewing the rag.

He leaped to his feet, taking that milk bottle with him, and when I crawled upright, I held my hickory club.

I met him head on, holding the club like a bat. He feinted with the bottle; I just swung hard at his exposed head. If it had hit him, we would have buried him. I wasn't fooling around. Neither was he. But he brought the bottle up fast and ducked his head. The bottle shattered on the culvert wall, but he still held on to its jagged-edged neck.

He lunged at me, the shining glass held like a dagger. I leaped back in balance, but right against the curved concrete wall. I swung the club with all my weight behind it, but I was too close to the curved side and it jolted out of my hands. Ray lunged again. I ducked. He came closer; I hopped back. Now he had me cornered against the lowest arc of the concrete culvert and smashed the jagged-edged bottle neck into my naked nose. I went down screaming, my hands to my face, blood pouring between my fingers.

"C'mon, yuh little bitch," and I could hear them running.

I might have bled to death if Angelo Ferrara hadn't happened along to share the fire for the night.

He stanched the flow of blood with a handkerchief soaked in wine, cleaned the wound, murmured soft words to me, half Italian, half English. Then he stoked the fire, fried some bacon, made hot coffee, helped me sit up, stuffed bread and bacon into my mouth, held the cup of coffee for me. The pain was deep and sharp, but I ate. Not a word. Dawn was approaching. He put out the fire, cleaned up his gear, washing everything with wine from an earthen jug, stashed everything in his knapsack. Then he examined me again. His fingers were strong and knew what they were doing.

"Lucky kid; you could lose eye. Not too bad now, maybe you have a little scar. Your nose broke long time anyway. . . . What happen?"

I just shrugged.

He didn't press it. His eyes were small, brown, smart, sunk deep in his bullhead. His cap was shoved back and I could see he was mostly bald, a mere stubble of brown-gray hair. His thigh muscles bulged through the khaki work pants as he sat on his haunches, his shoulders were broad and heavy, his neck thick, and a blunt nose jutted out of a furrowed leathery face. When he opened his mouth I could see crooked, nicotined teeth. He looked like one tough son-of-a-bitch.

He let my eyes finish examining him, then grinned and said, "My name is Angelo Ferrara."

I couldn't figure this guy. He'd fixed me up, fed me with his own hands, all like it was in a day's work, that's all. I looked at him warily, a little worried. What did this old geezer want? He stuck his tongue into the inner part of his upper lip and just kept staring at me with those small brown eyes.

What the hell did I have to lose? "Max Miller," I finally said.

"Thank you, Max, I appreciate the favor." He stood up, he was a big guy, a real heavyweight. Hung his knapsack from his shoulder, picked up his jug of wine, and headed for the culvert opening. The gray dawn was turning yellow at the edges. Just before he left, he turned. "I go to Saginaw to look for work—wanna come?"

Stupid kid that I was, I didn't answer right away and he walked out. Move, you jerk! I picked myself off the ground and hauled ass. "Okay, Mister, I'll go wit' ya," I yelled as I hit sunlight, the pain in my nose a screech. He was already sliding into his pickup truck.

With a snort, drily, he said, "Kid, I hope you not a big pain in the ass."

I gave him a lopsided grin.

Ferrara sat hunched over the wheel, his cap pulled back on his bullhead, and he was whistling an aria. I didn't know it was an aria then, that took me sometime to learn. I was turned in my seat, my eyes traveling over the inside of the truck. A variety of tools of every description: an old-fashioned handcranked Victrola, the famous little dog and all; record albums of what I later learned were Italian operas, Beethoven quartets, Handel's *Messiah*; several books in Italian, one by Malatesta, the anarchist philosopher, one by Ignazio Silone, *Bread and Wine*; blankets, cooking and eating utensils, the knapsack, the jug of Italian red—all neatly stacked so each item was easy to hand. A rope line was strung from side to side from which hung recently washed longies, a work shirt, some towels, socks. An old single-barreled shotgun. Two hundred-pound sacks of sand. This guy was neat and clean, I appreciated that.

The tin flivver was going faster than any old pickup truck had a right to go. Turning to the old man, I said, "How the hell do yuh get this tin heap to go so fast?"

He laughed proudly and I could see his stained teeth. "I connect a high tension magneto from a tractor to the engine. She can go eighty. That way I screw Mr. Ford."

"I get it. Those sacks of sand keep her on the road."

"Hey, you pretty smart kid."

I smirked.

He stepped on the gas and the flivver hit sixty-five, and we rattled along, the sun behind us like a fried egg somebody hadn't the good sense to eat.

It was early spring. As I stared out the window, I saw farm houses and barns pass by swiftly: a farm woman in a sheepskin coat throwing a pail of slops to some pigs; farmers plowing, some by horse, some by old tractor, turning the not yet thawed earth; a young boy buttoned to his ears coming out of a barn carrying a steaming pail of milk; snowbanks melting, muddy patches near barns and houses; a wood sign nailed to a tree at the entrance to a dirt road on our left which read NEW DAY. I wasn't too dumb to smile.

Soon we were in Saginaw, farm town, factory town. I was surprised at how angry Ferrara became when he found the factories closed. I thought he had to be an idiot not to have expected it. Later I found out he just thought you had to keep looking, that's all, and only people who had given up stopped being sore about closed factories. He drove to three, four plants, all the same story. Chained gates, a sign: NO HIRING. Then he did give up and we drove into the center of town. It was still early morning. Shopkeepers were beginning to open their stores. Horse-drawn wagons filled with sacks of grain wheeled past and old pickup trucks, one with several pigs, another with heifers. Idle workers strolled in pairs, alone, some leaned against storefronts. FDR's optimistic smile lit up many windows. Ferrara pulled up in front of a diner and treated us to coffee and. 20¢. I said, "Thanks"; he said, "*Niente*, nothing."

As we left the diner, I tripped on my broken shoes and torn spats, and Ferrara caught me before I hit the deck. My nose felt as if the bottle were still stuck in it up to its neck. He looked me up and down—my tattered jacket, my see-through pants, my so-called shoes. Shook his head. I started to get mad, but he whipped me around and pushed me ahead of him into a Monkey Ward's nearby. As I went in before him, he stopped a moment, took out some dollar bills from his pocket, counted them, again shook his head, shrugged his huge shoulders, and followed me in. I didn't ask any questions; he was in charge.

Later we stood at the curb near the flivver, I all decked out in new work shoes, khaki work pants, with the blue denim collar of a new work shirt blossoming out of a brand new gray sweatshirt. I couldn't figure this guy. He wasn't rich, only an itinerant working stiff. What was up with him? I'd met some nice guys on the bum, but, shit, nobody like this. Before he headed for his side of the car, I put my hand on his arm to stop him. "Whaddyawant from me, Mister, buyin' me all this stuff?"

Ferrara pursed his thick lips, whistled a bar or two, then, to my surprise, asked, "You go to school, Max?"

"Sure."

"What grade?"

"Tenth."

"That so? You learn how to read?"

"Of course. Real good, too, I'm no dummy."

"You are educated boy, better educated than more than half the world. More than me. But you talk like tough guy in movies, you think it make you look tougher than you be. To me you just a kid, an educated kid, do not try to scare me with tough guy talk—or I whack your ass hard!"

He looked like he meant it so I kept my mouth shut, after all, I had a good thing going, why spoil it? So we slid into the truck and were soon out of town on the same two-laner. Again we passed the sign, NEW DAY, this time on our right. Again I smiled to myself, if this sucker wanted to feed me and dress me then it sure was a new day. Ferrara caught a glimpse of the sign, too, pursed his lips, then lowered his eyes, and began to whistle an operatic aria. He seemed to know millions of them.

After a few seconds, he said to me, "You look like honest kid to me. If you stick with me, you work, save money, pay me back for new clothes, okay?"

Well, that was a little different. "You bet," I said. "I'm no bum, I'll pay my own way."

Now he added, "You will teach me how to speak English good and I will teach you how to live decent . . ."

"Aw, don' gimme dat shit!"

He was driving very fast, but took his hands off the wheel and turned to me with a cocked open hand. I thought for sure he was going to clout me. The car swerved sharply. Without a twitch of a muscle, I said, "Better watch out."

He grabbed the wheel and righted the car. We were hitting over seventy. He observed me from the corner of his eye. "Maybe you *are* tough kid."

I registered my victory by gingerly feeling my wounded nose. He pulled out two sticks of gum from his breast pocket and handed me one. I nodded. "Thank you very much, Mr. Ferrara."

He burst into laughter and I joined him.

The bill of his cap high on his knobby forehead, me leaning against the door, we both chewed away as the tin heap hit eighty.

A map of the North Central States. An old WPA mural—the kind painted in new post offices by WPA artists. (You know the kind, leftwing or liberal realistic proletarian painters.) A miniature flivver pickup truck speeding along a narrow meandering road: fields of corn and wheat from horizon to horizon, flanked by a huge farmer on one side and a giant worker on the other, shaking hands over the rippling gold.

Angelo drove fast. We spoke little or much, as we pleased. Days we worked, if there was work to be found. There was nothing Angelo Ferrara couldn't do with his hands. Taught me the difference between a carburetor and a piston; how to hold a paint brush so it did its share of the work; a hammer—"Let tool work for you, kid, that is why some genius invented it"; how to drive a tractor—it was easy; harness a team of Belgian drays; to roof a barn. We made two bits, half a buck, sometimes even a buck a day. Many days we made nothing. Kept a glass jar in the back of the flivver to hold our coins. Once it was all filled up, a few times it hit bottom. But we managed to eat and I paid him back for the clothes he'd bought me. The son-of-a-bitch, I thought he'd say forget it, but, like hell, he took it and bought himself a new record, Verdi's *Requiem*. He was generous, but not made of mush. He made me pay my share. It was spring, then summer; we began to live off the land. Berries, a rabbit—the old shotgun worked fine—vegetables, a loaf of bread, a pail of milk or a slab of pork earned working for a farmer or storekeeper in town. They were no richer than we, though we were both better off than those who lived in the big cities. Factories were closed or half closed; shops were empty, bankruptcy notices tacked on doors; evicted families sat dejectedly on their old furniture in the street.

Nights we camped under a tree off the road, made our food on a fire, handcranked the old Victrola, listened to *The Barber of Seville, Rigoletto*, a Beethoven quartet, Mozart, Monteverdi, or read a book borrowed from a public library. (Returned next trip, "If you steal a little, soon you steal much.") Rainy nights, I slept curled up like a cat on the front seat, Ferrara under a pup tent.

I was no longer a bindlestiff. I worked, saved a nickel or a dime, had a friend. I cared for him—he cared for me; he wasn't just being kind to a kid on the bum.

We made our way up two-laners to Lake Michigan, followed it south to Gary, Indiana, little work, around the horn to Chicago, none at all, north into Wisconsin, Milwaukee, Madison, La Crosse, north to St. Paul and Minneapolis, Twin Cities, across the Mississippi, headed south. We worked, we were idle, we drove. It hardly made any difference where—the country was skidding on the balls of its ass. Thirty or forty million people scrounging for a dime. FDR smiled optimistically.

Saw milk poured into rivers because in the market place milk was greater in supply than demand. The hungry can't pay. Wheat, barley, rye burned for the same reason. Supply and demand. NRA. WPA. PWA. CCC. Relief.

Driving, Ferrara whistled his arias. I dozed, talked a blue streak. About home, the old block, my mother and father, Archie, Elsa, the kids. Angelo said little about himself. Came from Dearborn, Michigan, was on the road about as long as me. Before that Milan, Italy. In '21 he'd blown up a fascist meeting hall. Five men died. Fought terror with terror. A bad way of life, kid. He was an anarchist. Comrades helped sneak him out of Italy, il Duce's police on his trail, followed shortly by his wife Carmina and little daughter Angelina. They'd had an older son who'd died of typhus. America. U.S.A. Worked for Ford Motor Company. Ten years on the fuckin' line, kid. His daughter married, left immediately for San Francisco. Bad times arrived. Left Carmina, hit the road with his truck. Why? No answer, clammed up. His business, not mine. He never asked me to tell him more than I wanted, I never asked him.

Nebraska, Kansas. Wheat and corn fields as far as the eye could see. Harvested. Burned. Too much bread on the market. Garbage Cities overpopulated with moneyless, starving men and women. Helped the economy. Into Missouri, followed its river into St. Louis. Saw demonstrations in the streets. Neighbors banding together to put a stop to evictions. Crossed the Mississippi again into Illinois. Angelo jumped out of the car, waved his cap and did a jig as we watched farmers with shotguns stop the foreclosure of a destitute farm. North to Springfield, Illinois, jumped the Sangamon River, the Illinois, up to Moline and Rock Island. A few factory chimneys churned smoke. Bridged the Mississippi again to Davenport, Iowa. The glass jar was three quarters filled. Angelo took two bucks and dragged me to a symphony led by a blond geezer called Peterson. Angelo sat entranced. I fidgeted and dozed.

Recrossed Old Muddy, headed southeast to Peoria. Factory smoke in the sky. WPA. PWA. CCC. Union organizers at plant gates. Police clubs hammered their heads as Ferrara stormed. We worked the farms. Harvest time. Jumped the

Wabash into Indiana again, raced north to Fort Wayne. An auto plant's stacks were alive. Less unemployed on the streets. FDR grinned. Hit the road, workless days—it was hit and miss. The glass jar was almost empty. Made a hit. Ferrara repaired six tractors. I plowed. Whizzed across Ohio into Pittsburgh, its night sky smoldering red. A few steel plants had reopened.

Backtracked into Ohio, hit Akron, Toledo, were almost in Dearborn, Angelo's home town. "Shit," he said, "we go to Kalamazoo." Kid that I was, I shrugged, didn't even wonder about it. Kids are stupid, especially when they think they know it all.

We worked, we ate, went a little hungry. "Maybe we work way to California, visit Angelina and her bambinos." No, not yet, something drew him back to Michigan, and then something drew him away, he never said what. "Okay, no California." What difference did it make to me? I was on the road. Had run away. He made me write to my mother. (I hadn't written except the first couple of weeks after I'd jumped the line. Why? No excuse—I was just a mindless, cruel kid. Now I'm being repaid. I got married when I was forty, the war, too many things intervened, so my children are still young and my middle boy, Peter, has copped a beat. Now I know how it feels myself.) Elsa answered to General Delivery, Ann Arbor. That was our home base—where Ferrara received his mail, an occasional letter from Angelina, but mostly an Italian anarchist newspaper called *il Martello*, *The Hammer*. Elsa said they were managing, were alive. She worked for the Federal Theater Project, wanted to be an actress. Mama worked as a milliner. The kids were growing up. When was I coming home? Ferrara and I were a good team, why should I go home? We ate good, we worked hard when there was work to be had. We camped nights, Angelo listened to music, I read books.

I was tanned black as a Zulu. I was almost seventeen and as big and strong as a grown man. Angelo kept looking toward Dearborn, but we never went. That was his business, not mine. Owosso—unloaded sugar beets at the sugar plant. Saginaw again. Flint. Lansing. St. Charles. Ames. Tecumseh. We worked more frequently, the glass jar was almost filled to the brim. Angelo said in the fall, after the harvest season, maybe we'd return to Wisconsin, to the lake country, for fishing and hunting. Then he'd go to California to visit his daughter and grandchildren and I'd go home. I told him I'd go where I pleased, they didn't need me at home. Things weren't that much better, you could eat one day and starve the next. I'd just be another mouth to feed. He retorted that my life was aimless, I was going nowhere fast. I told him it was no different for him. He shrugged, pursed his lips. We were driving fast on a two-laner which lay straight as a rule between Paw Paw and St. Joe. The fields on either side stood tall with corn in the lavender dusk. I stared hard at him. Bemused, he raised his dark, heavy, gnarled hands to look at them for some reason with his small, wise eyes. The car swung sharply and I told him, "You're gonna kill us one of these days."

I liked this old guy. Why should I hesitate to say it? I loved him, and I'm sure he loved me. We were kind to each other. That means a great deal.

In that culvert, that deep cave, he'd peered hard at that broken-nosed, cynical kid and had seen what he'd seen, then decided this was a human being he could save from slipping into hell—he was a missionary, goddammit—and hell to Angelo meant living without hope, corrupted by despair and so broken, not merely by accident of environment and the circumstance of history, but by loss of will to resist. When I told him how hard I'd tried to resist taking advantage of Tillie's sadness for me, her kind wish to give me a gift, he smiled proudly for me; when I told him that when I swung that hickory stick at Ray's head it was with an intent to kill, he shook his head sadly, unhappily. I only understood much later that he was telling me he understood only too well. But then he went on to berate me, to attack the killer in me, in me specifically, but in himself, too. I must say this: I was on the verge of leaving him plenty of times. "Fuck you, Ferrara, I'm tired a yer sermons." Of course, I didn't really mean it, and he knew it, but he'd urge me to stay because he knew I loved hearing it.

Aaa, hell, he was a strange guy, who touched everything with his thick fingers, smelled everything with his blunt nose; there was nothing he wasn't curious about. He had a quick fuse which he managed to muzzle mostly, and in those days I thought he was a patsy, a dumb jerk. Christ, he couldn't say no to any con man on the bum. There was something else in the man, something I felt akin to, though I couldn't figure out what the hell it was, an unhappiness that would catch him in mid-stride and send him flying off into some horrible fantasy that made him grimace with pain. I never heard him cry for himself—that's not true, once I did, and it hurts still to think of it—or bemoan his fate. He laughed at death, and I can only believe it was because he enjoyed being alive . . .

I say to myself now in my own old age, you've made a myth out of him, he wasn't all that good, when he farted he stank, sometimes his mouth smelled so bad from the butts and the wine you had to open the flivver windows and keep your head turned; there were days when he was so sunk in on himself that he ignored every word you said and when you screamed at him for it he'd blow his fuse and look so cruel you thought you were going to have to fight for your life. Yeah, so what! He was Angelo Ferrara and he saved your life—that's what. Okay, just remember he was no angel from God. All right, jump the line, get on with it.

We were back in Michigan. We were saving our dough for that vacation trip to Wisconsin. It was still harvest time.

Dusk. The tin can barrelled along. We passed a sign reading, "Ann Arbor—8 miles." Angelo said, "Maybe we catch a movie in town tonight. Tomorrow we see if there is mail in post office."

"You never get anything but your lousy little Arneekist newspaper. Solidarity forever . . . the union makes us strong. Horseshit!"

"Cut it out, kiddo, or I whip your ass."

The flivver swerved, was righted. "Please excuse me, Brother Ferrara . . ." We both laughed. "Maybe there's a Harlow movie. Boy, could I stuff her."

"You go with girl in St. Charles last week."

"I'm not an old man yet, Angie."

Sighing, "You bet . . ."

"Cleo Gordon . . . what I used to do to her on the roof."

"You know, Maxie, the chickens do it, the cats, even people do it. What there to boast about?"

"Okay, okay."

In Ann Arbor that night the movie marquee read, "GARBO IN QUEEN CHRISTINA." I loved her even more than Harlow. So did Ferrara. I could never stand that John Gilbert, though. Alongside Garbo he was as stiff as a wooden duck.

Before we slid back into the truck after the movie and sundaes at the Sweetheart Ice Cream Parlor, Angelo said that we'd camp outside town and I agreed.

"I know who I'm gonna dream about . . ."

"You know what, kiddo? Me too!"

Under a bright white moon, the flivver stood squarely and solemnly off the road at the outer perimeter of a giant weeping willow tree. We half sat, half reclined under its rustling canopy as the Victrola played Verdi's *Requiem*. The flames brightened and warmed our faces as Ferrara rolled a cigarette and I whittled on a stick with my penknife.

The choral voices made the night tremble. I don't know why but that night the music really moved me. Up until then the records Angelo always played had been pleasant, after all I wasn't a savage, only a barbaric kid. Perhaps this time I really listened, perhaps it was the pure beauty of Garbo's face working on me, so I permitted the music to fill me up. I wasn't aware it was happening, but suddenly I felt enveloped by the beauty of the music and by a terrible lonesomeness. I must have sobbed out loud, because Ferrara raised his eyes to me, and then quickly lowered them. I kept whittling away at the stick, but inside I began to crumble. Maybe it was the melting ice inside dripping drop by drop, each as it struck the walls of my belly splashing and running in rivulets through the accumulated dirt and debris. As the *Requiem* moved to its glorious end, I was overcome with grief and began to sob openly, without shame, and I could feel my shoulders shaking violently. The fire flamed up, and somehow I managed to look at Angelo and saw that his blunt face was captured by a silent, contained sadness, too.

The music came to an end and the needle wavered back and forth on that last tragic note as we merely sat there.

I cried, just cried. Tears must weigh a hell of a lot more than one thinks—or, maybe, there are so many tears in a man's head that even if one by one tears weigh very little, totalled they weigh a great deal, for as they begin to stream from your eyes, the weight of them hammers at you, buffets you, beats you so you tremble, the escaping sobs abrasive and sharp. I don't know how long I cried, but Ferrara didn't stop the record, the needle continuing to waver off and on the last note, until I cried the last tear.

Then he slowly rose to his feet, and through the tears I saw him, a fragmented bear of a man, stop the Victrola.

We both sat silently. I had by now regained my composure and was gazing sadly at my old friend. Then we spoke quietly.

"Lonesome, I guess."

"You think of your mama?"

"Yeah. Mama, the others, the old block, the pushcarts, the street games. Papa and Archie—the whole works. Don't you ever get lonesome for Dearborn, your wife, daughter, friends? Christ, it's so close and we never go there."

He firmed his thick lips, released them, shrugged, rotated his hands until his palms faced upwards, dropped them.

"Sure, Max, but what I got left there? My daughter go to West Coast with her husband. There is no work, Ford shut down, things get very bad. I lose myself, fight with my wife like it her fault. Carmina, she a fine woman. Fuh! I fall into inferno, become like an animal. I even beat her, whip her. Why? All go bad. I become rotten inside. The men not even want to organize—give up. Like you say, the sky open up and the shit come down. Nothing left for me but the garbage in the pail. I run away like you. Best for Carmina, best for me."

I shook my head in disbelief. "I can't see you that way."

Ferrara eyed me sadly. "Angelo is wrong name for me. I no angel—just bindlestiff like you. On the move, afraid to go home."

I still couldn't believe it. "A guy's not a biff if he doesn't give up and has a friend who means something to him. . . . I can't believe you did anything bad in your whole life."

"Fuh! You are a child. Believe me, I am like all other men—half animal, half human."

We sat in silence and I could see he was looking into his past, and now I know exactly what he was seeing. I can see the pain and horror on his face.

A working class kitchen—old-fashioned sink, black iron coal stove, chipped porcelain-topped oblong table, old wooden kitchen chairs, worn red linoleum on the floor. Angelo towers over Carmina, still a handsome woman in her mid-fifties, with angry dark brown eyes in a dignified face. She holds her ground as Ferrara shouts furiously at her, waving his heavy arms wildly. Suddenly he lashes out at her and she falls heavily to the floor.

I stared at him, asked shyly, "She go with another guy?"

He shook his head. "You are a child, think everything has to do with sex. Nothing like that. Things are very lousy, no work, the poor do not want to do anything for themselves, men not want to organize. . . . Aaa, I cannot blame the bad times, Max, not all. That too easy. Other people not go bad like me. I must blame myself. I become nothing . . ." He smiled ruefully, shifted the conversation from himself. "You have a good cry, eh?"

"Yeah, it made me feel better."

"That's good," he said, climbing to his feet and stretching sleepily. "Time for bed. In the morning we go back to Ann Arbor, pick up mail, then look for work. Another couple weeks maybe we have enough so we can go to Wisconsin lake country. We travel much, work hard when there is work, now we have a good time, eh, kiddo?"

"You bet," I replied, smiling happily. I fetched the blanket rolls from the truck, we removed our shoes, and soon were lying on our backs in our makeshift beds.

For many minutes I lay there, my eyes examining the intricate patterns the willow branches and the white moonlight and the banked fire flames conjured up in my imagination. Though Ferrara was a few feet away I could feel him waiting—the wise old coot knew what I didn't know, that there was something I wanted to tell him. I shifted to my side as if I were going to sleep. He didn't move. All of a sudden I was on my feet and standing over the old man, staring down at him. He merely observed me with his wise little eyes.

"Don't laugh at me, Angelo, but I gotta tell you something."

"You know I won't laugh, kid."

"I got these terrible feelings . . . damn . . ." I had to stop, feelings and thoughts were rushing into my head and made no sense and I had to stop.

"Take your time, Max. Just say it straight, how you feel, how you think."

". . . I got this feeling I wanna tear the world apart, smash things, you know what I mean? I see my mother, my old man, too, taking their beating. Before I fall asleep I always see Archie dead in his coffin and Elsa crying and the little kids, Davie and Sarah, screaming, their eyes like holes in their heads . . . the garbage and the rats and the lousy food when there's food. . . . Sometimes I stop to count all the garbage cities I've been in, and they all look the same— garbage dumps, big piles of garbage with rats, and I try to remember how different people I met looked and they all look alike, skin and bones in rags eating off the garbage. I see Tillie looking at me sad, a scared little bimbo, and Ray . . . Jesus . . . Ray screaming with pain when he saw her with me . . . and I'm swinging my hickory stick, wanting to kill him because I wanted her too. I get so mad I feel I'm going to explode. Smash things, beat up on the world. It keeps going through my head like a plowshare ripping up my brain. A fist's in my belly full of power, ready to let go. . . . In town I see the girls in the street and they look soft and smell sweet and I think how they look naked and I feel I want to bury myself in them, sweet and soft, and they're kissing me with their eyelashes and everything's good . . . clean and good. Then I feel great and I wish I had the power to make the whole world happy, give every bastard all the food he can eat. . . . I feel like two men—one good, one bad. But I tell you the truth, most of the time I feel like a piece of shit and I want to die . . . yeah, that's it, want to die. . . . It's hard to explain, goddammit, but that's how I feel. . . . Tell me the truth, for crissakes, am I nuts?"

Slowly Angelo sat up, and his eyes on me, he said, "You not crazy, unless you try to fool yourself, find good excuse."

"Quit crapping me and tell me the truth."

"I ever lie to you?"

"No, I don't think so."

"You know what you are, Maxie?"

"What, c'mon, tell me."

The old man raised a palm, smiled kindly. "Just a goddamn fool man, Max—that's all, just a man . . ."

Just a goddamn fool man, that's me.

The very next morning we returned to Ann Arbor to see if there was any mail. For Ferrara there was his latest copy of *il Martello*, but no letter. He was hoping and waiting for a letter that never came. He tried to conceal his disappointment, but I was beginning to be able to read him almost as well as he could read me. I received a letter from Elsa full of news about the family. They were doing all right and of course she asked me to come home—"Mama says please come home, there's plenty to eat." I folded it back into its envelope and slipped it into my pocket. We left the post office and walked to the flivver. As I was about to get in, I saw the tailgate was open. Ferrara waited as I went back to close it. Before lifting it, since it was unusual for it to be down, I looked into the back. The glass jar with our money was gone.

I yelled at Angelo and he came running. Frantically our eyes searched all about the area—we hadn't been gone for too long—and down near the end of the block we saw someone running, the glass jar shining in his clutched hand. I ran, Ferrara after me. Whoever it was ran straight, didn't try to duck into a side street, ran without looking back. I really moved, left the old man behind, began to catch up with the guy. If he'd ducked, I'd never have caught him, he was too far ahead, but he didn't, he was a homing pigeon, straight as a rail he ran until he reached an old rundown house, turned without stopping, ran up the wood steps and through the door.

It wasn't a house—merely the pretense of one. Maybe once it had been a house. Every window was broken, doors hung on one hinge, no furniture, old smelly newspapers spread around like someone had slept on them. An old deserted house that tramps and hobos sometimes used to spend a night in. I'd slept plenty of nights in houses like that before I met Ferrara.

Let's make it brief, it hurts too much. I found the guy all right. And his wife. And his two kids. They were in what used to be the kitchen. An old sink, a couple of orange crates for furniture, old newspapers for bedding.

They crouched in the corner when I slammed in, the four of them. Black sticks, they were. Black skin gray. Black holes under their foreheads. Crouching in the corner behind their bony knees and rags. A rag would have been proud to be called a rag in that company. People, for God's sake! I have to say I wasn't moved too much by the sight of them. I had seen so much of it, I was hardened to it.

"Give me my money," I said. I wasn't mad now, I only wanted my money. Ferrara and I had worked plenty hard for it. I had a callus for every buck in that jar. Through the rags and gray-black skin five bones stuck out holding the glass jar. Four gray-black skulls and eight dull black eyes stared out at me. I grabbed the jar just as Ferrara clomped in, breathing hard.

"I got it," I said. "Let's go."

Angelo didn't move, merely stared at them. Bit his thick underlip. Reached out and took the jar from my hand. Placed it on the sink. I can still hear the clink of glass on porcelain. He turned to leave, bidding me to follow with a nod of his head.

If he'd asked me, and he should've asked me, it was as much mine as his, I'd matched him minute for minute to earn that dough, if he'd asked me maybe I'd have walked out with him. But I doubt it. I'd been on the bum too long. Poverty didn't move me much, other people's, that is, I'd been too hungry long enough.

"Like shit," I said. "Half that money's mine."

He stopped in his tracks—those four pairs of eyes were on us, they were holding their breath, I guess—he was already halfway out the doorway. Now I could hear them breathing fast.

"You don't understand, kid."

He wasn't being fair, goddamn him. "It's half mine," I repeated. Once the machine starts, it's hard to stop. Angelo stared at me with his little brown eyes—contempt, that's all. Drowned me in it. I wanted to say a word, any word, but couldn't. He raised the jar, spilled out bills and coins, stopped when it was about half-empty, handed it to me and walked out.

In a bloody haze I followed ten paces behind him all the way back to the flivver. My head was dizzy with anger at his unfairness, with fear, with contempt for myself—but the stinking machine kept working and I couldn't stop it, I was cursing him under my breath. He stepped into the cab before I got there, started the motor, and left me standing at the curb, the glass jar in my fist.

"SUCKER!" I screamed after him. "SUCKER! SUCKER!"

He was gone. It would have been better if he'd never seen me again. Better for him.

There were thirteen, fourteen bucks left in the jar. Don't smile. That was a lot of money. A smart biff could live a long time with that kind of coin. Hard-earned coin, too. I could live a month easy on it without doing a stitch of work, or even stealing or begging. With the whole jar we'd been planning to have a great time, Angelo and me—eat steak, live off the fat of the land for a while. Now he was gone. Fuck him. Patsy. Sucker. Just a bloody preacher, that's all he was.

I put away a big lunch. Pork chops and two helpings of applesauce, a half loaf of bread, two big chunks of pie a la mode and two cups of coffee. I was sixteen going on seventeen and could eat a whole cow. With the tip—80¢. I farted around Ann Arbor all afternoon. Whistled at the university coeds. Ate a huge supper, steak and french fries, more pie a la mode, more coffee. Went to the movies. Can't remember what I saw. Didn't see a thing. Something was missing, felt empty inside. Missed Angelo Ferrara, the big son-of-a-bitch. Old dago bastard. Sucker, just a stupid soft touch.

I left the movie house. Went to the whorehouse at the edge of town. That money in my pants pocket was a curse— every cent of it. Wanted to get rid of it, that's all. Shuffled around town, hoping Angelo had returned. The machine was running down. Went back to the Sweetheart Ice Cream Parlor, one of the old-fashioned kind, marble tops and wire-backed chairs, filled with college kids. Had a banana split— couldn't eat it. Damn him—whyn't he ask me, I'd have been glad to give those poor people the dough. Yeah, now I would. Started to leave. Some wise ass big guy wearing a sweater with a big "M", football player, big man on campus, showing off in front of his girl, a sweet titted, red-headed girl, made some remark about my broken nose, I don't know, but those sitting with him looked at me and laughed.

I went up to him, told him to stand up. He did. Six feet of football muscle. I hit him so fucking hard he bounced when he hit the floor. It felt damned good. Got rid of some of the heat inside of me. But now I faced three more geezers with "M's" on their sweaters. You want to know the truth, I was beginning to enjoy myself. One of them came at me, his hands up thinking he knew what he was doing. I feinted him with my eyes, he followed, the jerk, and I canned him with a combination he never saw. I turned to the other two. I'm not boasting, remember, I was trained by one of the greatest fighters of our time, and a well-trained pug is just too much for two, three plug-horses off a football line. This time they came at me together, one high, one low, and I had to stiff-arm one and plant a right hook on the other. It was beginning to look like a battlefield, as other big "M's" started coming at me from all sides, and now I knew I was going to get bombed myself, when I felt myself picked off the floor and wheeled around.

It was Angelo, and I couldn't help laughing. "You kids," he said to them, "go home to mama and papa before this tiger eat you up."

As we got into the old flivver—home, sweet home—he said, "Tiger Max—you should not a fight amachures."

"When you going to learn? You should not fight amateurs."

"*Grazie*, kid. *Grazie*."

The flivver rattled out of town doing seventy. We never discussed what had happened earlier that day.

That was the end of it.

The next morning we headed for Saginaw. I didn't ask him exactly where and he didn't say. I was happy to be with him again, that's all. To my astonishment he turned the tin can into the dirt road at that old wood sign: NEW DAY. We'd passed that sign ten times coming and going on the Saginaw road and never even stopped. I swiveled my head to ask him about it but decided not to; he was gritting his crooked teeth and I didn't want to bother him. Wherever he took us was all right with me.

The truck bumped along the potholed dirt road under a long canopy of trees. It had the quality under there of a cathedral, quiet, solemn, and the sun sifting through the leaves gave it the feeling of stained glass windows.

We continued rattling through the sun-splashed darkness, then emerged into a magnificent landscape of thousands of acres of wheat, barley and rye undulating gold under a gentle southerly wind. From the distance we could faintly hear the throb of a stationary thresher. The gold stretched into the horizon, melting into the sun.

He was smiling now, so I asked him. "How come we never stopped here before?"

"First we have a little bite, eh?"

We ate an early lunch of cheese, bread, and Italian red under a stand of young chestnut trees. Then as I munched on an apple he told me about New Day Farm. A hundred or so families, anarchist comrades of his, had got together, pooled their resources and bought the farm at depression prices from the Owosso Sugar Company. ". . . Ten thousand acres. They come from New York, Detroit, Philadelphia, from all over country. Everybody call it something else—commune, collective, kibbutz. Men and women, old, young, work equal, the best each one can. Everyone get equal shares of food, shelter, clothes. The children go to communal school, are teached—"

"Taught."

"*Grazie.* . . . Taught by teachers who belong to the commune. At night the children live with their papa and mama." I was lying on my back, but I was listening. "It is not perfect, that for sure. They are people, and people even when they come by their own will disagree, fight, become mad, some work harder than other, some lazy. They human, a wife look at another woman's husband, a man look at a friend's wife. They live close together, though each have their own room, but everybody know when you shit, bleed, snore, cough, have family fight, make love. They try to make life equal—food, clothes, roof over the head—but people never equal. Some smarter, some dumber, some strong, others weak, and the strong always find way to boss the weak. But maybe they will win and learn to live together because the beauty be stronger than the ugliness. I not fool you, Max, I do not think they will endure. Not yet. They are a tiny island in a big and very rough sea. But it is by their own will, that is very important. Because they try, I have much respect for them."

Ferrara lifted the jug of wine and took a long pull. The sun was rising higher by the second, that gold out there shimmered, it was hot. I sat up and asked him, "Then why don't you join them?"

He set the jug on the ground, thought a moment before answering. Then he smiled. "I never know why I pick up a smart kid when I can pick up dumb one. That is good question, because you know I believe in everything they do. But I also believe a human being who thinks like I do cannot live outside the sea and make believe it not there. He have to fight."

I thought before I spoke, and when I did it was gently. I wasn't out to hurt him. Perhaps I was beginning to learn—a little, anyway. "Then why are you on the road, Angelo?"

He gazed at me with a sad smile. "'You are a smart boy, and good one when you want to be. I am glad I come back to look for you."

"I'm glad, too."

"To get my strength back, that is all. When the right time come, I return to the fight." He stood from his haunches.

"Now it time we go to work. That old thresher is missing on one cylinder and drive me crazy. You hear it?"

I listened. Merely heard the low throb of the motor, so I cupped my ear. "Yeah, there it is. You got an ear like a bird dog."

He began to clean up camp and I watched him. "Say, Angelo," I asked, "why didn't we come here before? We passed that sign out there ten times."

He hesitated, and I sat up, observing him as he placed our things in the back of the truck. "They are my friends," he said. "They hear about me and Carmina, that I act bad with her. I was ashame to look them in the eye. You understand that?"

"You bet." I slowly rose to my feet and joined him in the cab of the flivver.

In a few minutes we had parked near several old trucks and were leaning against a fender, shielding our eyes against the blinding sun. In a corner of the huge field squatted the thresher still missing on one cylinder, blowing chaff through its stack like a rain of gold. The thresher was being fed from a wagon drawn by a team of giant Belgian drays, their hides glistening tawny, another team impatiently pawing the earth as they waited their turn. Out in the field were a good dozen teams and wagons being loaded by farmhands, and in the distance the tops of a stand of stately oaks swayed gently in the breeze.

As Ferrara stood admiring the scene, I eyed a tanned girl in khaki shorts and red blouse who was one of a loading crew throwing sheaves of wheat on a wagon as it made its slow progress down the field. Her face, as were all the others, was black with field dust, streaked where the sweat ran. Her hair was bunched together under a red scarf. She had a plump, nifty tail, and her legs though sturdy were very shapely, sexy even though she wore heavy work shoes. She worked with an easy rhythm, following alongside the wagon, never missing a beat. When one of the wagons out there was fully loaded, it headed back for the thresher, and the crew started loading another empty.

As we were standing there—I think Ferrara was afraid to move, that's the truth of it, afraid to meet his old friends— the thresher motor coughed, then stalled. We stared in its direction and I said it would be a good time to break in, they'd be so glad to get their machine fixed, they'd forget all about him and Carmina. He playfully slapped my head and muttered, "Smart-alec," under his breath.

As I guessed, they were so happy to see him, they practically kissed him. Smiles, affectionate slaps on the back. A lanky gaunt-faced guy, wearing glasses on a nose like a Turkish hookah, who seemed to be in charge, looked up from the engine and without even a hello said, "Just like you, Angelo, not to show up for a year and then come when we need you. What about it?"

Ferrara shoved him aside and without even looking said, "I fix it quick, don't worry." Then he introduced me to the man—his name was Irving Green—and the guy told me to join one of the loading crews, any one of them would be happy to have another pair of hands. I did what came naturally, I joined the crew of the girl with the nifty tail.

The other members of the loading crew were two young guys, a middle-aged woman, two middle-aged men. They all nodded to me without stopping their work. One of the middle-aged men, as plump and round as a ball, greeted me with a big toothy smile. "I never saw you before, Brother, but sure am happy to meet you now." The others laughed, and I joined them. I positioned myself behind the girl, I sensed she was about my age, and guessed that behind the field dust she was pretty. About her bustiness there could be no doubt, nor that her teeth were small, even, and very white when she smiled at me as I took up my station behind her lovely ass. My face was soon as black as theirs.

As we made a turn, the thresher started, its motor singing. Ferrara was a wizard, and I smiled, but the rest of the
crew and those all around the field stopped a moment and
cheered. Angelo worked at the harvester now, loading bags
of wheat onto a truck.

We loaded our wagon, started another, stopped as a water
truck approached. Tin cups of water were passed to each of
us. Cool and fresh as a pine forest. The girl and I stood
together.

"Dina Dumashkin," she said.

"Max Miller." We shook hands.

"Have you come to live with us?"

"Oh, no. I'm with Angelo Ferrara—the guy who fixed the
thresher. He sure made it hum, didn't he?"

"Are you related to him?"

"Just friends. . . . You live here?"

"Of course. We came from Philadelphia last year. . . .
Where you from?"

"New York. But I've been on the road, bumming, you
know what I mean."

"How long you going to stay?"

"The day, I guess. Do you like it?"

"We work awfully hard—yes, I like it, but I miss the city,
too."

The chief loader stood on top of the wagon. "Back to
work, comrades."

We worked another hour or so, loading wagon after
wagon, the field was forty acres, that's a lot of wheat. Just
as I was beginning to realize I was starving, a truck began to
make the rounds, dropping off sandwiches, fruit, tin cups of
hot coffee. The crew continued to work, stopping only
when the food truck approached. Once the wheat's cut, you
got to thresh it before a heavy summer rain comes along to
rot it.

Each of us received two sandwiches of ham and cheese, a

large tomato, half a muskmelon, hot coffee. As the truck left us behind, the roly-poly and the middle-aged woman ran and jumped on the tailgate. One of the young guys who'd been working opposite me muttered something nasty under his breath. The chief loader turned on him, "You'll be older yourself some day, and the young and the strong will do your work."

"Yeah, at this rate, I'm going to become old before my time."

Dina and I sat side by side, eating, talking. To get me to move my eyes from the young fellow, she said, "Being on the road sounds adventurous."

I stared at her. Was she kidding? "We work, we eat. If we don't find work, we eat less. But we've been doing pretty good since harvest time began."

"Aren't you lonesome for your family?"

Nosy dame. I didn't answer.

"Aren't you?"

"Sure."

"Why'd you run away?"

I observed her blackened face and saw her eyes were sad. "Why the . . . why are you lookin' at me like that?"

"Because you look very lonesome." She had the same sad eyes now that Tillie had that night under the culvert.

Dames. . . . "I'm not lonesome with Angelo. When I was on the bum alone, I was—and hungry, too."

"You look like you're still lonesome to me." Involuntarily she touched my hand and it was like an electric shock, my head spun.

I smiled at her. "When we finish the field, will you go walkin' with me?"

Dina raised a shoulder, smiled at me with one corner of her luscious mouth. "When we finish, I'm going back to the compound, I'm going to take a shower, then I'm going to get into something clean and cool, and then I'm going to the mess hall and eat and eat. Then maybe we'll take a walk."

"Is that a promise?"

"We'll see," she said with a smile.

We were silent as we faced each other and my heart was singing. She was legit, I was gonna go with a girl that was legit. The chief loader called us back to work. I stood up first and she lifted her hands to me and I helped her to her feet. As she came off her behind she brushed against me and I held my ground. She laughed merrily and the sound of it almost made me lose my breath.

We worked our bloody asses off, but we finished the field, only then were the horses sent off to their stables, and we just flopped on our backs to await the trucks.

Angelo and I got cleaned up in the communal shower room, and then we ate a huge meal of borscht and pork chops and big chunks of bread and salad in the communal dining room, and then he went off to the nightly communal meeting and Dina and I went for a walk . . .

That's it, bud.

History, circumstance, life—call it what you will—being what it is, I never saw Dina again, that is, not for twenty years or so when I was "introduced" to her by her husband Sidney Dubin, a colleague of mine at the union. She was— is—still very beautiful. I had never forgotten her, nor she me. Sidney stood with his mouth open as we laughed and embraced and kissed. She told her husband and I told Becky. Her daughter, Kathy, and my son, Eli, became lovers at the age of thirteen, believe it or not. They're still friends. We were all hoping they'd get married, but I don't know if it's in the cards. Kathy's a cross between her mother and father, a lovely young woman, and Eli, though he and I have our troubles, is a great kid, but, of course, I'm his father and prejudiced. He's rock honest, still a bit wild at twenty-three, with his mother's face and she's a smash—her good looks and brains, my strength and bad temper. Life's strange— right? Right.

We left New Day Farm that night, Angelo and I. I'd have stayed, been happy to, but not Ferrara, he had other things on his mind. He was waiting for a letter that never seemed to arrive. There's no sense keeping it a mystery—it did come shortly thereafter. I wish it hadn't. My wishing something hadn't happened after it did is a self-indulgence, like giving yourself a cheap squeeze.

So we left New Day, at least on the surface a utopian paradise—for those who came, spent a euphoric day captured by a desire to see the future, and then left before the hardships were revealed. Like slumming in reverse, vicarious, an emotion easily bought. Ferrara knew that for those who stayed it was a difficult, grinding life, having to decide each moment of the day how much to withhold of themselves from the collective and how much to yield up. Nothing in this life comes easy—nothing at all. And those who come up with easy answers to every fucking human problem are only blowing hot air, the kind of hot air that can kill. If you stayed at New Day Farm a day, a week even, you thought they had it made. They didn't. They broke up a couple of years later, to return to the cities they'd come from, to the work they'd left—sewing, pressing, union organizing, carpentry, every trade, even that of making money in the capitalist system.

Angelo and I found work. The harvest had come in heavy. Times were a little better. FDR kept smiling. The unemployed rolls went down a bit. There were fewer biffs and bims on the road. Our glass jar began to fill up again.

Three weeks later and autumn blew in. Ferrara and I plowed all day. The farmer we worked for generously offered us his hayloft for the night—mostly because he wanted to show off the electricity just installed by Rural Electrification in his house and barn. He even had a radio.

Burns and Allen. The Spider. Eddie Cantor. Fireside Chats. Amos and Andy. Fred Allen. And the moon came over the mountain.

Sitting under the single light blub at the end of a wire, the smell of fresh hay in our nostrils, we ate our supper. Angelo began to hone a chisel blade on a sharpening stone, and I, sitting in my BVDs, to sew a button on my pants fly.

In the middle of nothing, his eyes intent on his work, Ferrara said, "Maybe the time come for you to go home to visit your mama."

Startled, I pricked my finger. Sucking blood, I looked at him.

"Why not? You know you miss her and your family."

I still didn't say a word, and he continued honing his blade.

"Think of your mama, she must be worrying plenty about her son."

"Just when I'm beginning to feel good, you start that crap."

"Hold your temper," he said, honing away. "I talk to you like a man, you answer like a child. If you not go home soon, you never will . . . you keep running away for always. Let life lead you 'stead of other way round."

I knew he was right, had even been thinking about it myself, perhaps that's why I got so mad that I threw the pants down and jumped to my feet, my fists raised in anger.

He merely continued sharpening the chisel blade. "Take it easy, Max."

"You made a promise we'd go hunting and now you're backing out."

He raised his little eyes from under his cap. "You better sit down before you do or say something you be sorry for. The time come for you to control yourself."

"Oh, shit," I shouted, leaning towards him. "You and your goddamn preachin'—just when I'm beginnin' tuh feel clean for da first time in me fuckin' life—"

Calmly, his eyes still raised, he said, "Speak English."

"Spik Inglis yourself."

"Shut your mouth fast, kid!"

I blew. "Yuh nogood dago bastard—"

He was on his feet, red in the face. "Never say that to me, you little—" I raised my fists to him, but slamming down the chisel and stone, he grabbed hold of me quicker than a wink, bent me over his bulky knee and simply whaled my ass. Hard. His hands were made of iron. I flailed about like a netted fish. Finished, he threw me on a bale of hay, resumed his seat, and again began to sharpen the chisel blade.

He paid no attention to me as I lay there glowering. Pursing his lips, he examined the blade under the light bulb, then stored it away in his knapsack, the stone as well. He hesitated, came to some conclusion, withdrew an envelope, a sheet of stationery, a stub pencil and put them on the bale next to me.

"All right, Maxie. I am sorry I push you too hard. You win. We have enough money soon and we can go to Wisconsin. Find paradise. Maybe next week or so. But after that you have to think about going home for a visit and I go to West Coast. A month later we meet in Ann Arbor and go on like before. You write to your mama that you come home real soon, eh? Tell her you are healthy, eat like horse, shit like bull, and you with old man who be damnfool enough to think he can teach stupid kid like you anything."

Before I could tell him that now I knew he'd been playing games with me, that this is what he'd been aiming at all the time, he began to descend the loft ladder.

"I go to buy some cigarette makin's."

I almost laughed, the old bastard. "You're full of it, you're going to visit that farmer lady near the Corners . . . she's been keepin' a light lit for you for days."

"I am free man. I go where I please."

He had stopped, his head still showing, and I couldn't help smiling at him. "I am *a* free man—when you goin' to learn?"

"Smart ass."

His head disappeared, and I was already writing home when I heard the flivver start, go into gear, and speed off.

That night, it can't have been any other, there is a meeting in Louie Sica's house in Dearborn. By now I've been at a thousand meetings in my life, maybe more, so I have a pretty good idea how it went. The meeting is held in the kitchen—a big old-fashioned kitchen with torn dirty wallpaper, one window pane broken and covered with cardboard, a black coal stove on which a large black-sooted coffee pot simmers. Over the stove a line's strung wall to wall on which hang diapers, towels, family underwear. The floor's covered with worn brown linoleum patterned to simulate parquet.

Around another chipped white porcelain-enameled table—nearly every working class family in America had one in those days—four men sit drinking coffee from assorted cups. The cigarette smoke is dense; the ashtrays overflow.

Ida Sica, Louie's wife, moves in and out of the room as the men talk. She's in her late thirties, tired, haggard, once a beautiful Italian girl. She wears a gingham dress. Her breasts are large with milk. And she looks awful sore.

One of the men at the table is Louis Sica, a thin nervous wiry man with great energy, about the same age as his wife. He's the only one there who went to college and he's wearing metal-rimmed glasses to prove it. He and the other men are wearing faded blue workshirts. They've earned them. The other men are Scotty, a little man with sandy hair, younger than Louie, his face ice cold—a tough cookie, a real action-action guy, he never believes he's anything but right, exclamation point; then there's Kovac, an open-faced burly blond man in his mid-thirties, strong, intelligent, a man with a conscience always at the surface, not hidden; and Murphy, a slender redhead of twenty-eight, with quick eyes which never stop flitting from face to face, a wise guy to hide his ignorance.

The meeting's about over. Louie, a leader of men, is tired, has heard enough and is ready to rise.

". . . Okay, then . . . it's agreed. No date set, but sometime next week. Get to work, but try to keep the loudmouths quiet."

Murphy, his eyes running from face to face, smirks. "There's always sure to be a canary."

"Just let the word out that canaries can't sing without tongues!" That's Scotty.

Kovac sighs and shakes his head. "We gonna start that already?"

Louie stands, and they follow. "We don't have time for that talk now. If someone's going to talk, he'll talk. If we have the men with us, we'll win . . . that's what it depends on, that's what it always depends on. I'd like as little rough stuff as possible."

"Fat chance!" Scotty again, his eyes ice cold.

That's the end of the meeting. They leave. Louie sits down and writes a letter to Angelo Ferrara, General Delivery, Ann Arbor, Michigan.

Deeply engrossed in a book, I didn't hear Ferrara when he returned. As he reached the top of the loft ladder, his shadow loomed large over me and I was so startled I jumped out of my skin and grabbed up a pitchfork stuck in a bale. My own movement was so fast and precipitous that

Angelo himself was startled and almost fell back through the ladder opening. He had to catch himself and the cigarette that dropped from his lips.

"Whew! give a guy a break. First you scare the shit out of a man, then you're going to burn him to death."

"*Scusi*, Max. What you reading?"

"*Les Miserables*. That son-of-a-bitch Javert—"

"I know," he laughed, "you already read that book three times and tell me."

Laughing, too, I stepped to the opening at the end of the loft, under the block and tackle for lifting hay, and began to urinate. He joined me, and we were quiet for a moment as we listened to the tinkle down below.

"How your ass feel, Mr. Tough Kid?"

"I bet it feels better'n your hand."

"That be profound truth, boy. Your ass like stone." He boomed a loud fart.

"Gowan, you—you—" and I boomed one in reply.

We were both laughing as we turned into the loft, adjusting our flies.

"Let us hit the hay, kiddo." BOOM!

"Okay, you old—" BOOM! BOOM!

Raising his hand as if to whack me, he exploded a fart to make the barn shake.

I lifted my leg and detonated a couple myself. "If you—" BOOM! BOOM! "—wanna have a gas war, you better—ha ha—ditch that lit cigarette." And I laid a fart that lifted the roof.

I was now rolling on the floor, and Angelo was dancing up and down, both of us hysterically laughing and farting, so that in the house Mrs. Farmer's new radio crackled with static.

The following day I mailed my letter, telling my mother I'd be coming home in a month or so, and then we hit it good with a farmer who had three, four days of work for us—painting, plowing, corn binding, shoveling cow shit. We put in ten, twelve hours a day, made twenty cents an hour a piece, and came away with thirteen bucks clear after food. We decided that while we had it we better go to Ann Arbor the next day for mail and then head for Wisconsin. Both of us were happy—we were well-fed, healthy, rich as Ford himself. We also decided we would work our way to the Dairy State so we could have enough money to buy ourselves new pants, shoes, shirts for our respective trips. I was going to hitch home, so I didn't need money for the bus. Angelo also said I ought to have enough to buy presents for my family, and I told him I knew, he didn't have to tell me, I wasn't a barbarian, I was a civilized man, and he laughed. A week before that would have been enough to start a war.

I was surprised to find a letter for me—special delivery—and I ripped it open. They were so goddamn happy I was coming home, I almost cried. Then I noticed Angelo's face. He'd received a letter, too, marked PERSONAL, underlined in red. He hadn't opened it, was merely staring at it, his eyes wide, excited. He nodded that we leave.

He didn't tear it open until we sat in the flivver, then read it with deep concentration, with nearsighted squinting eyes. I was certain it was from his wife. To keep my eyes off him, I reread my letter. Suddenly, Angelo started the car, and we left the town behind doing eighty. All the while he's muttering in Italian, but he hadn't said a word to me and I was a little miffed. His blunt nose was twitching and his eyes were shining like black buttons. He seemed to be totally unaware of me. I had an idea it was bad news and I got scared.

A few miles out of Ann Arbor, near Tecumseh, parked under a tree off the road, he slid from the cab without a word, and holding the letter as far as he could from his eyes, he read it again, squinting, making sure he got every word.

Finished, he began to tear it into tiny pieces; as he did he saw me as if for the first time, and his troubled face changed to dismay.

"Oh, *scusi, scusi,* I so busy with my letter—"

"That's all right."

"You not mad?"

"Why the fuck should I be mad?"

"I so—"

"What's so important about it?"

"First tell me what your mama say?"

"That they're happy I'm coming home—what else?"

"Buon, buon."

"Well, what about your letter?"

He couldn't seem to look me in the eye, and I was getting more worried by the minute about the Wisconsin trip, which seemed fated never to come off, but I held my water as he got our lunch out of the car and we sat down to have Italian salami, bread, fruit, cheese, and wine. As we began to eat, he finally looked me in the eye.

"We go to Dearborn."

"Dearborn? Why? We're on our way to the lake country."

"Friends organize to fight Ford. Company won't talk to them . . . they goin' to make him talk. They need help. I have to go."

I didn't understand then, only much later, but this was the excuse he needed to send him hurrying back to Dearborn to see Carmina. Not that he wouldn't have gone back to fight Ford, no excuse necessary, but he could tell himself this was what he was waiting for, not Carmina. He just wouldn't admit to himself that if he didn't return, Carmina would by need and choice find another man soon. He'd been gone more than a year. Young people never seem to realize that older people have as great, if not greater, need for the opposite sex as they do, not only out of loneliness, but for love and sex, preferrably with one and the same person. Now that I'm old myself, I understand about him and Carmina. Then I didn't understand a damn thing, I was only a dumb, selfish kid, so I said, "You go to Dearborn—I don't give a crap about Ford . . . or your friends either."

"You no give a crap?" He shouldn't have been surprised, but I guess he was too excited to think straight.

"No, I no give a crap—I'm sorry, I didn't mean to mimic you." (I knew it drove him crazy when I did.) "Let's go to the lake country . . . what about your daughter?" I was trying to get to him, but it didn't work.

"When friends call for help there is no time for pleasure."

"They're not *my* friends."

"You no have to do nothing. Just wait for me in Louie Sica's house. They need me in the beginning, then we can leave and do what we decide. The world not come to an end . . ."

I was upset, couldn't eat, stood and paced around.

"You listen to me, Maxie. This against Ford—the big one—the king. He give when he want, he take away when he want. Every working stiff is supposed to kiss his ass. My friends want to make it equal—fifty thousand men equal one Ford. Not a great big advance—but better than nothing. Me and my friends wait for this long time. We just want to make him talk to organizing committee. . . . Come here and sit down, I want you to recognize me, too." I did as he asked. "What you afraid of?"

"Goddammit, I don't know."

"We are poor working stiffs, right?"

"Yeah, right."

"Take all the crap, right?"

"Right."

"When things get bad, who suffer the most?"

"We do."

"Now we have chance to give it back."

"In the end they'll win—the big guys always win. You're a sucker, that's all."

"Can I never get through that thick head—?" He threw up his hands. I saw he was torn in two—by my demands, by his own demands. He'd given me a lot—

Oh, shit. I'm getting old, sentimental. Cry easy. Forgive me. You can cut it out of the tape—or leave it in, I don't care. I'm not ashamed.

He'd given me a lot, it was time I gave him something.

"Okay, Angie," I said. "You win. We'll eat Ford up—give him the old one-two."

We scooted toward Dearborn at our customary high speed. Only once did Ferrara lift his hands off the wheel and have to catch it before we crashed into a tree, and that was when for no apparent reason he threw up his hands and whooped for joy. He was perking inside like our old coffee pot on a hot applewood fire.

We arrived in the city at twilight, and passed the automotive plant where he had worked. It was a huge sprawl of brick with dirty smokestacks, a few of which spouted black soot. Only half lit. A high steel mesh cyclone fence enclosed it, a double gate in the center of each of its four sides. Behind each of the four double gates stood a guard booth, and I took a gander at the uniformed guards. The plant resembled a fortress.

A few minutes later we pulled up in front of Louie Sica's old frame house held together with wire, string, and glue. Night had fallen and some lights shone through the windows, one covered with cardboard. When Angelo joined me on the sidewalk, he pointed to a small darkened house across the street. "My house where I live with Carmina and my daughter . . ."

I glanced at the house, then at him. His lips were pursed and he was whistling under his breath.

"You going to see her?"

Sadly, he shook his head. "If she let me I sure want to see her. She is the only woman I ever love."

We passed through a wood gate hanging lopsided from one hinge, narrowly avoiding an old baby carriage and several garbage cans. The house looked like it would fall apart in a breeze. "Sonuvabitch Louie always hate to work on house—too busy organizing . . ." We arrived at the back door simultaneously with a pair of metal-rimmed eyeglasses on the bridge of a banana nose stuck into the upper third of a long, thin head. The eyeglasses stared at us through the window in the door, and suddenly we saw a mouth smile. The door opened and Angelo entered, I behind him. The man held a shotgun which he immediately leaned against the wall. The long thin head must have rested on strong shoulders otherwise they would have caved under the pounding of Ferrara's heavy hands. Then they were hugging and kissing in the European style. Angie. Louie. How a you, kid? *Buon. Buon.* Maxie Miller, my friend. A friend of Angelo's a friend of mine. Hiya, Louie.

And we were in the kitchen being met by the others with shouts of affection, especially from Kovac. "Hey, Ferrara, you old coot."

Again I was introduced, and we all shook hands. Scotty. Murphy. Kovac.

Ida Sica was there, too. She and Angelo embraced warmly, and he kissed her hard. "We sure have missed you, Angelo."

He patted her behind and Louie yelled, "Hey, what the hell . . ."

Ida laughed. "That's a man's hand—not like yours, you skinny rooster."

We all laughed—me, too, drinking in the scene. I was in a friendly home—it felt good, I'd forgotten what it was like.

Soon all the men, including Angelo and me, were squeezed around the kitchen table. Ida brought the newcomers hot soup and cups of coffee. Before she left, she said, "Not too loud, please, I have children sleeping. And give my husband a break, he hasn't slept in nights."

They talked, I listened. I was with Ferrara, not with them. As he spooned hot soup, Angelo asked, "What the score, boys?"

Louie spoke for them. "The plant's been open for a couple of months. Half the men are working . . . but the line's moving faster and faster, a man hasn't time to scratch his ass. The faster it moves, the fewer men they need. We say slow it down so a man can take a breath and hire more men. But they won't even talk to us. The men are pretty sore . . ."

"We're going to close the gates and keep them closed until they talk to us!" Scotty, of course.

"It's set for—" Sica started, and Kovac interrupted.

"Sorry, Max, but—" The guy was embarrassed. I was a stranger; they didn't know me.

"Maxie's a good boy—you can trust him. He is my friend—like my son." Angelo put his arm around my shoulder, and I smiled at him.

I saw Scotty's cold eyes on me, and I challenged him, who the hell did he think he was? We held it for a few seconds, then he said, "The kid's okay!"

"Thanks, bud."

Kovac smiled—he was the kind of guy you like as soon as you look at him the first time. "No offense, Max." I nodded at him, and Sica finished his sentence.

"It's set for Wednesday morning, three days from now, seven o'clock whistle."

——— 59 ———

"All the men for it?" Angelo asked.

"My section's one hundred per cent!"

"Not mine, I'm sorry to say. Fifty-fifty, I guess."

"That's because you're too soft, you dumb Hunkie. . . ." Murphy smirked.

They all laughed—not Angelo. "Shut up, Murph, that the kind of joke I never appreciate."

"You always had a thin skin, Ferrara. . . . My section'll be out—all of 'em."

"You hope!"

Louie Sica, the leader, had no time for chitchat. "We don't know how many goons the company'll have. If it's only the guards at the gate, it'll be easy."

"No chance! Their security boss has men all over the place. They'll probably know and be ready for us. Rough! It's going to be fucking rough!"

"That's the way it always is," Sica said drily. "Once you beat them and they recognize you, then it's easier. Right now the men want the dignity of an answer. You can say the company has been our best organizer. The men who were called back to work were so damned happy they wouldn't even talk to me. The company believed it would be a good time to increase the speed of the line. Faster and faster. More and more production. They overdid it . . . then spit in our faces. They told me they could get a million men off the street to take our places . . ." He sighed. "I'm tired . . ."

They took this as a signal to leave. Before they did, Murphy said to Angelo, "You gonna be in my gang? We can use a bear like you."

"Thanks, Murph. I go where Sica tell me. Maybe I stay close to him—he so skinny he need me to hold him up."

Everyone but Louie laughed—leaders never seem to have the time to laugh. "Come on, get out of here."

After the three of them left, Louie led Angelo and me to our room. Two broken down beds, an old bureau, and a chair. "The crapper's down the hall." And he was gone; the man could hardly stand on his feet.

As Angelo and I undressed, he told me that he should warn me that the going would probably be very rough at the plant and if I didn't want to be part of the strike action, I should say so. I told him I'd stick with him and not to worry, I was able to handle myself, as he well knew. He acknowledged that fact, and we went to sleep. We slept late—till eight o'clock, when we usually rose at dawn. We were in beds, broken down, it's true, but beds.

The days that followed moved fast. Briefings, a gathering of the troops, a battle, a war. Lessons, endless lessons. A man died—two—maybe more. As soon as I looked in one direction, I was forced to turn on my heels and go in the opposite.

It was like a documentary movie—*cinema verité*. Black and white.

Lights! Camera! Fast music!

The Sica kitchen. Morning. The sun's so powerful, it gives the wear and tear an antique sheen. The Sica baby's crawling around in a makeshift playpen in one corner. I'm tightening loose cabinet handles with a screw driver and Angelo's sitting on a window sill, feet inside, body out, scraping old dried putty from an empty window frame. As he scrapes away he whistles an aria from *Tosca*.

Ida Sica enters carrying a large wicker basket of dirty clothes which she empties into a galvanized tin tub boiling on the coal stove. She stops to wipe the baby's nose, then stands hands on hips before the window, observing Angelo at work. One of my eyes is watching my own work, the other is on her. Her face is sharply lined in the bright morning sun. She seems unhappy, bitter.

Angelo stares at her, stops whistling. "What's wrong, Ida?" She shakes her head, bunches her lips, ponders a minute. They are, of course, separated by an empty window frame. Angelo resumes scraping out old putty.

"They all just returned to work, what's their hurry? We started putting some food into the children's hungry bellies. All the women are angry, not only me. Why don't they ask us for a change? They want the boss to talk to them, but they don't talk to us ever."

Angelo's working very carefully, making sure every bit of dried putty is cut away before installing the glass pane he bought, which leans against the wall near his feet. "You know who you marry, Ida, he not fool you. He is a man who will never breathe easy until every human being is treated with dignity, justice." When he says the word, it sounds like "joostice." "You not—"

"When you're hungry, you have very little dignity, you know that . . ."

Angelo sighs deeply. "*Si*, I know it very much."

"We want bread, we want love, we want attention . . ."

I've finished tightening the handles and now go to the kitchen door which hangs loose on its hinges. I begin to unscrew them in order to reset them. I am all ears.

"Yes," Angelo says quietly, "life not move in a straight line, it curl like a whip and leave scars. More pain than happiness . . ." He pauses, he wets his lips, and I know he's embarrassed, shy. "You have seen—huh—how is—?"

Ida knows what he's asking. "Yes, Angelo, I see Carmina occasionally. She's all right, works a little." It's obvious she's unhappy at this turn in the conversation. She can't manage to look at Angelo. The twelve o'clock factory whistle blows and she uses it to change the subject. "Have you heard from Angelina lately?"

He has caught her hesitation, but answers. "We write each other—not too much, but we keep in touch. You know how children are, they forget the old folks. She have two babies. After me and Maxie go to Wisconsin for a little vacation, I go out there to visit her."

As the door swings loose from its frame I have to step into the back pantry to grab it, and she thinks I won't hear her, so she says, "Where'd you find the boy?" But my ears are wide open.

"On the road. Poor kid run away from home. Same old story. Nothing to eat and he cannot stand to take food from his mama's mouth. He have a hard time—become like a wild animal. I think I help him become human. But he help me, too . . . lonely, getting old. He think I am angel . . . great man . . ."

I catch a glimpse of her soft smile as she says, "Angelo Ferrara, you are a good man," and inside my head I smile, too.

The old coot beams with pleasure at her words and I am glad for him. Now I'm working inside and out with the door, having some difficulty with it, but I notice as she turns away. ". . . Have to make lunch for the children."

But he has slipped under the raised window and grabs her arm. "Ida?" Unhappily she turns back to him, observes him sadly—he's trapped her, I can see, and I sort of expect his words. "What's the matter? What you hiding from me?"

My work slows down to a walk, I listen, can see she's resigned to telling him. After all, he's a grown man. I also see his face is white with foreknowledge.

"Something hard to tell you, Angelo. Carmina is living with Riccardo Giambatista. She seems happy. You've been—"

I stop working to look and listen. He stands there like a steer that's been dazed with a sledge hammer before slaughter. His face has that terrified look that Ray had in the culvert when he woke up and saw Tillie wasn't at his side. Ida has raised her hands palms up, is biting her lips, her face full of grief for him.

Two children gallop into the kitchen, a boy of eight and a girl of eleven. They see Angelo and run shouting to him, leap on him, hug and kiss. He has to respond, and does so heroically, kissing them, too, holding them hard to his chest.

Ida sets out lunch for the kids and as they leap to the table Angelo slips from the room and I can hear him walking to our bedroom. I resume hanging the door. Ida remembers to introduce the children to me. They smile shyly and I wave to them.

In front of the house I'm repairing the wooden gate and looking through the window of our bedroom. Angelo's pacing back and forth. I stop working and sneak in closer to observe him. He's breathing hard, having difficulty catching his breath. His agony is profound, and inside myself I'm crying for him.

In the kitchen, Ida's at the washtub, scrubbing clothes. The house is silent. The baby's asleep in the playpen.

It's late afternoon. I work around the house. Angelo hasn't left the bedroom. I go to the door, open it a crack. He's standing in the middle of the room, his head in his hands, his shoulders quivering. Suddenly he pounds a heavy fist into his callused open palm, doesn't stop; he pounds harder, louder and louder, and it sounds like someone shooting a clip of bullets in a forest.

Gate 1 of the plant. Almost dark. Behind the closed double gate armed guards stand ready to throw open the gates.

The plant whistle blows. Working stiffs begin to emerge from the factory doors and the guards fling the gates wide open. Several workers walk together, tired, dead beat. One of them says, "Glad to get outta there. It's a hellhole . . ." He does an imitation of Charlie Chaplin's imitation of him.

Another worker who isn't amused says, "Hell has to be better'n that. See you at the meetin'."

A third worker heaves his shoulders wearily. "I dunno . . ."

That night. The Sica kitchen. Several workers enter. Angelo and I sit at the table with Louie Sica, who is tense, nervous, speaks snappishly. "Let's get going, I have four more meetings tonight."

The men sit around the table—all dead serious, nobody's screwing around. Louie Sica begins to speak, "The time has come . . ." Next to me, Angelo rises to his feet and slips from the room, my eyes following him. He hasn't spoken four words to me since Ida told him the bad news. ". . . It's our job to keep the gates closed. No one's going in there till the company sits down and talks . . ."

I keep staring at the door, waiting for Angelo to return.

Same time. A basement. Scotty's talking to a filled room. "There'll be plenty of goons and scabs, so come prepared to fight! We have to keep those gates closed . . ."

Same time. An old-fashioned neighborhood grocery store. Twenty or so workingmen stand around, sit on the counter, on barrels, crates. Kovac's on his feet. ". . . Gate 3, that's us. We'll have another round of meetings tomorrow night, and that'll be it."

A young fellow named Pearson stands. He's smooth-faced, with a little nose and very clear blue eyes. "Kovac, you guys are crazy. I bet yuh don't get fifty per cent a the men to stay out. Everybody just began working . . . the women are sore . . . we need a couple more months at least . . ."

Kovac nods. He's an honest man. "I agree with you,

Pearson. We need six more months. And in six months we'll need another six. The men are mad, that line's moving so fuckin' fast yuh can't see it. If they slow it down, unemployed men'll get work and employed men'll be able to breathe. There has tuh be a beginning—now's the time for it. The boss has got to learn to talk to us. So we'll teach 'im."

Another man stands, about thirty, with glasses. Martin. "I agree, too. But we're doin' it ass-backwards. We oughtta take the plant over and kick the boss's men out and lock the gates from the inside. We'll give the plant back when they talk to us and treat us as equals. We should never forget the plant belongs to us. We built it and it's been run with the profits made off our backs . . ."

"You're right, Marty," Kovac says. "But not yet. The time will come for that. Now we have to show the company and the men, too, that we're ready to fight . . ."

The Sica kitchen. The men are shaking hands with Louie Sica as I slip through the door and hustle over to our bedroom. Angelo's not there! I run like hell to our flivver. The tailgate's open. And the shotgun's gone.

In the Sica bedroom Ida's patching a pair of pants. ". . . And the gun's missing, too. Where does Carmina live?" Ida jumps to her feet terribly upset.

"27 Decatur, the second floor." She tells me how to get there—it's a couple of blocks away.

I'm so scared my mind's blank. I'm running, that's all. Fast. Very fast. It seems like an hour but I must hit the street in ten seconds flat. 27. There it is. A two-story taxpayer. Lights on in the hall, voices yelling, Angelo's, a woman's, another man's. I'm expecting to hear a shotgun blast. Two steps at a time.

The door's open. Angelo's back is to me. His gun is cocked, his broad shoulders tense. Before him stands Carmina, her face white with anger, her jaw strong, her eyes blazing. She's fifty years old, and I tell you in my seventeen-year-old eyes she's a remarkable woman. Not so much the way she looks, but the way she stands in front of that fucking shotgun. And Angelo's straight, stiff, he looks like a giant, and by the set of his shoulders I can see he means business. Another man's standing near her, Riccardo, and he's as big as Angelo, about the same age, a decent-looking guy, and he's not scared either. I wait at the door, not knowing what to do, but ready to move. But she's taking good care of herself—not only with her eyes and face. I'd never seen anything like it in my whole life up to that time, and nothing like it since.

Ric is dying to get at Angelo, that's easy to see, but I'm worrying about the gun. Carmina says to Ric, her voice strong, tough. "This is my affair, not yours. You better go to other room." She speaks like Angelo. "I handle this."

Angelo takes a step towards them, and Ric raises his fists. "Just go!" she orders. "I not need him to fight for me, I not need you either." There are only five, six feet separating them now and I know that shotgun's loaded. Ric still hesitates, and she says very loud, "GET OUT!" Shrugging his heavy shoulders, biting his lips, Ric leaves.

Turning to Angelo, her angry eyes never leaving his face, she speaks very quietly. "Put the gun down." I don't think she ever saw me at the door.

"You kick me when I am down," Angelo says bitterly. "When I need you most."

"If you want to shoot me, shoot, but I not talk to you unless you put the gun down."

She beat that gun down with pure guts, that's what she did. He lowered it, and I sighed with relief.

Coldly, she says, "You not the only man in the world who lose his job . . ."

"I have a bad time. We have good life together, that not mean anything to you?"

"You whip me like a dog, I cannot forget it. We were not the only family who went hungry." Suddenly soft and sad, very quietly, she says, "Maybe you can forgive yourself, I can't. I am sorry."

"Carmina, please . . ." I cringed for him. So did she. Angelo's shoulders are shaking—he was crying for himself, and I was crying for him, too. I kept hoping they'd clinch and live happily ever after.

She's gazing at him, her eyes very sad, a beautiful woman. No patsy, the real thing. "You have to learn to have respect for yourself again, Angelo"— she said his name softly, it was almost like the sound of love—"and then maybe you will forgive yourself. Again be a fine, decent man."

He caught hold of himself, his shoulders stopped shaking, he stopped crying for himself, he was Angelo Ferrara again. They stare into one another's eyes, only their breathing is heard. Outside a car rips by. A dog barks. At that moment he has to speak. He has to tell her he loves her, that he has loved her his whole life, for what I see in her eyes is pain, ambiguity, and perhaps love. I don't know—I will never know. But he can't seem to find the words. Perhaps there are no words to express the pain, the shame at his betrayal of their love. What held his tongue? All he had to do was say the words. No, he couldn't find them when he needed them most. So what he did was make his admission. "You are right, Carmina. What else can I say? Live happy."

He took her hand now, her fingers, and she let him, and he kissed her palm. Her eyes stared down on his lowered head with great sadness, then her face simply smashed to bits, fell apart, but when he raised his head again, somehow her face came together again, only her eyes were sad, quiet before the grave of their long life together. There were no words they could find the courage to say, so they said nothing. I still waited, still sure they would fall into each other's arms, not understanding, but finally I, too, gave up.

I tiptoed down the stairs the way you do after the viewing of a dead friend, and soon I heard Angelo's steps behind me. Only then did I hear her crying . . .

The sun was very bright. Angelo was on the sloped roof of the Sica house, hammering shingles, and I was climbing up the ladder with a new stack of them. As I reached the top, I saw Angelo leaning against the chimney, breathing hard; he seemed to be in trouble, having difficulty holding on.

Eli Miller, my father, is sliding down the steep roof and I scream.

Quick as a cat I clambered to Angelo's side, held on to him for dear life. Scared, both of us were scared.

Finally, he caught his breath, relaxed. "Whew! Gettin' old, Max. Tired. Fuh! maybe it the sun. It sure hot up here."

"Come on down, we've worked enough today."

More or less normal again, he blew air through his pursed lips. "Finish the pile, eh?"

In a few minutes we were down off the roof and sitting on the tailgate of the flivver, our feet dangling, eating thick ham sandwiches and drinking wine. I kept my eye on him, though he appeared to be okay now. Suddenly he frowned and jerked his head around to his old house across the street. He clenched his teeth and stared wide-eyed. I know exactly what he saw.

The lawn is drenched with sun as a six-year-old Angelina and he play with a ball. Carmina sits in a canvas chair gazing happily at them. He gathers the child into his arms and runs with her to his wife, dumping the child on her lap, and then on his knees before them, he embraces them as they laugh.

"Let's get back on the road," I said to him. "Louie's got thousands of guys, what good are two more?"

"I am a little tired—upset from yesterday. But I feel good to be with my friends again, men I always live and work with—pick up my life again . . ."

"I tell you the truth, I'm scared."

"I understand that. You don't have—"

"You *don't* understand. I've got this lousy feeling . . ."

"What?"

"Oh, I don't know . . . last night . . . I want to get outta here."

He became impatient. "We have to do this. We do not live in paradise. It is necessary—for us, for our friends."

"You keep forgettin' these guys aren't *my* friends."

"*You* keep forgetting they more your friends than you know. What they do is for every man with grease on his hands. . . . We can't run away now."

I argued with him some more, I wanted to beat it, that's all. But he was his old self, tough, stubborn. His voice wasn't soft anymore. "You are in your heart a good boy, a decent man." If I heard that word decent one more time I was going to erase it from the English language. "But you have to stand on your own feet, and that you cannot do till you make peace with yourself, and you will not make peace with yourself till you stop running away."

"Okay, okay, goddammit, you win again."

The Sica kitchen. Night. Another meeting. Louie paces the floor. Scotty's staring out the window. Kovac and Murphy speak quietly to each other at the table. Angelo and I are playing rummy. It's 7:45 and in fifteen minutes everyone will leave for another round of meetings with the men.

The plant. Dark, except for lights in the guard booths behind the closed double gates.

A store loft devoid of furniture. The large windows at the front are painted black. The capacity crowd is lit up by a fly-speckled bulb hanging overhead. Kovac's speaking but is drowned out by the yelling.

"FUCK FORD!"

A large empty store filled to the corners with workers. Its storefront windows are blackened. A dismal blub hangs overhead. Murph's talking, gesticulating, but nothing he says is distinguishable because the men have risen and are shouting their approval.

Another large loft filled to the rafters. Windows are blackened. A bulb sizzles overhead. Angelo and I stand near Louie who's speaking calmly, coldly. "It's a matter of self-respect and good common sense . . ."

An empty warehouse crowded with workingmen. The crowd's unruly, jumping up and down. A fight starts and is quickly broken up. Scotty marches in and everyone is quiet. "I expect every man here to be with us. We're going to keep those gates closed so those who ain't with us can't get in. Once they can't get in, they'll be on our side. Then the boss'll talk to the committee man to man. Equals!" He receives a standing ovation.

A large service station garage. Crowded. Pearson, who was seen at Kovac's first meeting, is speaking. The men are very quiet. "I'm telling you they're nuts. We started working only a few months ago. . . . My kids are still so skinny I can count every bone in their bodies. If we had money in the kitty I could worry about my dignity. I ain't got no dignity when my family's hungry. I won't fight 'em. If they keep the gates closed then I'm stuck like everybody else. If they don't, I'm goin' through, boy, and you can believe it!"

The plant. Late night. Silent. Lights at the guard booths. Armed guards. A black limousine cruises slowly down the street. After it turns the corner, another black limousine rolls slowly and silently down the street.

"Why you do that, Max?"

It was early the next morning, gray, the flivver parked a few blocks from the plant which was barely discernible in the grayness. Angelo sat behind the wheel watching me wrap strips of rag around my fists.

"So if I have to hit anybody I don't break my knuckles."

"Remember, we do not fight unless we have to. Then you protect yourself as good as you can. The goons wear brass knuckles and if you go down they will kick you in the balls and head."

"Okay, don't worry, I can take care of myself."

Workers began to pass us on their way to the plant. A few, noticing Angelo and me, nodded. "I warn you again, this is not a game. You have to act responsible, not run wild."

I smiled at him and finished wrapping my fists, then began to slam first one, then the second fist into the open palm of the other. I tell you, I was scared. My mouth was dry and my asshole so tight you couldn't get a greased thermometer into it. I managed an okay, Angelo, sure, I'll remember.

But he wasn't through, maybe he was talking to give me time to calm down, maybe even time for himself to calm down. "One thing more. If the time come to run, we run— this is not a prizefight. We come back to the flivver and get away fast. *Capisce?*" I nodded and at last he said, "All right, kid, let's go." I managed to look him in the eye but couldn't manage to restrain the trembling which shook my bones. He placed those big sure hands on my shoulders and they felt damned good.

"Always feel that way before a fight," I said.

"I know," he smiled. "My stomach sound like harvester

missin' on one cylinder." You'd never guess, but as soon as he said harvester missin' on one cylinder my brain flashed the image of Dina and me heaving sheaves of wheat in perfect rhythm, our bodies one, our beat, our hearts, the sun slanting fiery red in the distance.

We joined a heavy stream of working stiffs heading towards the factory. The street blocks seemed extremely long. We all walked slowly. There was a great stillness in the gray morning except for our marching feet. It seemed to take us forever to reach the block on which the plant squatted huge, ugly, and ominous.

On the corner, Louie Sica was issuing instructions to a gang of men, directing them with his hands.

In the Sica kitchen, Ida sat at the table staring aimlessly as her infant sucked at her breast.

Louie kept sending the men coming at him off in different directions.

At the second corner, Scotty was surrounded by a large crowd. As were Murphy and Kovac at the third and fourth corners, respectively.

Angelo and I approached Louie. As we did, we saw Martin, the proponent of a sit-in, detach himself from Louie and slowly amble across the street where Pearson stood in the center of a large group of men. They appeared to be ashamed, but stubborn as Martin spoke to Pearson. Pearson shook his head, and, defeated, Martin headed back towards us.

"Not good, not bad," Louie said to us, "maybe fifty-fifty." He glanced at his wristwatch. "The whistle's going to blow in twelve minutes. Take this group and get going to your gates. Another gang's coming from the opposite corner to help you." I glanced in that direction and saw they were already moving silently towards Gate 1, our concern. Identical maneuvers were developing at the other corners, groups moving in on Gates 2, 3, and 4.

Angelo, myself, and the rest of our gang began marching towards Gate 1. Two guards stood behind the closed double gates ready to fling them open. Through the window of the booth I could see a third guard talking on the phone.

No one spoke. The sound of marching feet in the great silence was unreal, frightening. It was still early morning, gray, overcast.

Both our gangs approached Gate 1 from opposing corners. I could see the guards very distinctly. They wore guns on their hips and billy clubs hung from their wrists. It was their duty to open the gates and keep them open so that those workers who wished could enter.

As we neared our gate, Angelo said so we could all hear him, "Keep calm as you can. No rush, take it easy." Oh, yeah. My belly was doing backflips, frontflips, standing on its head.

A large black limousine filled with men drifted past us. Then another. A third turned the far corner and came down towards us. It drifted past. Followed by another.

We and our other gang were approaching Gate 1. The third guard stepped out of the booth and the three of them stepped forward to open the double gate. They were going to show us who was boss. As they tried to open the gate, four men from our second gang ran towards the double gate and snap, snap, one of them shackled his hands to the two gates and the center post. Two guards began to flail away at the shackles and hands with their billy clubs while our men tried to protect their comrade. The two guards were cursing with frustration as they banged away. I almost laughed. The third guard began running toward the plant. He'd return shortly with a hacksaw and attempt to cut the shackle chains loose.

As our two groups moved towards union, one of the limousines drifting past pulled over to the curb ahead of Angelo and me, and its beefy passengers piled out. They were dressed in civies and carried truncheons which hung from leather thongs around their wrists. A second limousine pulled up behind us, and again men piled out. They looked awful big and tough.

Similar events were taking place at the other gates. At Gates 2 and 4, men had shackled themselves to the center posts. Gate 3 was open and men were fighting with goons and guards.

Large open-bodied trucks with workers standing in the back passed us. The goons from the first limousine ran in our direction. I almost shot out of my skin. Angelo snapped at me, "Try to keep cool, Max. The old one-two, remember?" And I could swear I heard him laughing with pleasure.

Our two gangs joined, the double gate behind us, and we turned to face the goons who ran heavily toward us, clubs swinging from their leather thongs.

One goon went right at Angelo, but I didn't have time now to watch out for him. I was taking care of myself. The man was big, but he was clumsy. I had made my battle plan and was ready for him as soon as I heard someone take the first punch. As he swung his club at me, I ducked, grabbed at the leather thong and yanked with all my strength. The clumsy bastard was off balance and went to his knees. I rocked him with a hard right to the head. He shook his noggin and scrambled heavily to his feet, but he'd lost his club and I kicked it hard and it rolled to the fence. I remembered every lesson Punchy Goldstein had taught me in the gym. The guy was big and still acted like he was going to have an easy time with this kid, but I jarred him good, throwing combinations, giving each punch all my weight, keeping in balance, taking his punches on my arms and shoulders. I was working very fast and loose; the guy didn't hit my face once, and he was breathing very heavily. But I could see his face was murderous as he came bulling at me. I kept hitting him and soon he was bleeding under the eyes and in the mouth and he was bellowing to beat hell. The brass knuckles gleamed on his fists, and his heavy hobnailed shoes sparked on the pavement.

I could hear Angelo taking his guy near the steel mesh fence—the thud of his cannonball fists as they pounded flesh and bone. Others were fighting all around us, and the double gate was still closed. But one guard, his hands through the opening near the center post, held the shackled man by the throat while another guard sawed away at the chain.

I kept clouting my man, had him under good control; I was a professional prizefighter, and he was only a goon. His eyes were puffed and bleeding hard, still he kept flailing at me. Now my arms and shoulders began to hurt, those brass knuckles were ripping them up. If I didn't set him up soon, his weight and the knuckle dusters would wear me down. I kept setting him up and missing his jaw. Suddenly he clobbered me one on the mouth and I bounced on my ass, spitting blood. The man began to kick me with his heavy shoes, and I crawled away—the wrong direction, to the fence, and he had me plastered there as I climbed to my feet. I was taking the guy's punches on my elbows and arms, searching for a good clear shot to the jaw. Inside something broke loose and I felt free, murderous. Tiger Max. I wanted to get at this guy, eat him alive. But those knuckle dusters were ripping my arms to shreds and I could see him grinning as if he thought he had me.

Bleeding from my mouth, covered with blood, his and mine, still going after this guy, I heard Angelo call out, "Run, Max, beat it! I come after you." But I was past running. I wanted to get this man. I wanted to slaughter him and hang him by his heels like a quartered side of beef. I remembered his club near the fence and ran to it, scooped it up. Hefted it. It felt great. The man was after me, lunging for the club, his jaw wide open—a good clean shot. I whipped the club down hard. Could feel the crunch of it, the pain in him and the pain in me. As the man began to crumble, murder in me, murder pure and simple, I raised the club again and whipped his head with all my might, beat him and beat him, his shoulders, his head. I had broken loose at last; it was out in the open, all of it. I was on a rampage, berserk, for all of it, all the filth and stink and hunger, for my old man and my brother, for me—for me alone. Suddenly a strong hand grabbed the raised club and ripped it out of my hands. I turned in a rage—it was Angelo. His cap pushed back on his bald head, his nose bleeding, his lips screwed up so the blood wouldn't flow into his mouth, and his little brown eyes plunging like needles into my skull. He peered at the broken man on the ground, then at me. Shook his head, wrinkled his bleeding nose as if he smelled an awful stink, turned and started to run. "SUCKER!" I yelled after him. "SUCKER!"

Men were running; the double gate was wide open, and a steady stream of workers led by Pearson quietly passed through. The seven o'clock whistle blew—the whole mess had taken just twelve minutes. All the gates were open, our men were running, some were down, a bloody battlefield. Grimfaced working stiffs were jumping off tailgates of trucks and entering through the gates.

I wheeled and ran.

Angelo drove very fast.

I soaked clean rags with wine from the jug and handed one to him. Driving one-handed, he began to wipe the blood from his face. I did the same and then put a soaked rag in my mouth and bit on it to stop the flow of blood from my broken gums and lips. My face felt like a mashed potato and my arms and shoulders were raw. Angelo's knuckles on the wheel were gashed wide open, bleeding. As I unwound the strips of rag from mine I saw they were pink and tender but otherwise in fine shape. Inside I felt a little nauseous, and I could still see that goon's slack, broken jaw, his crumpled body on the ground. I had no feeling for the man. It had been him or me. I won.

Angelo stared straight ahead, stone-faced, his knuckles bleeding on the wheel, his body sort of shrunk in on itself as if he wished to be as far away from me as possible. I sat in the corner, nursing my wounds. The morning was now bright yellow. We were passing farm trucks, a few cars. Farmers were heading into their fields with horse or tractor. My mouth hurt and I refreshed the wine sop and stuffed it back in.

I stared at Angelo. Stone. He refused to acknowledge my presence. I began to get sore. What the hell had I done? Did he think I was going to let that goon beat the living shit out of me? It began to work on me. That goddamn unfairness of *his* need that I be decent, good, in the face of the mauling that guy had given me with his brass knuckles, his hobnailed shoes, his club.

It was too much for me. I spat the wine sop out of my mouth and yelled, "You fuckin' sucker. You think I was gonna let that bastard kick my balls in? I had to hit him, I had to!"

He didn't say a word for a few seconds; he was trying to control his own rage. The flivver was hitting eighty and rattling away. Just as I was getting ready to let go with another blast, he said quietly, "I tell you to run before. But I understand. I know you have to hit him. He deserve it. But I see your face and eyes when you slam him, and then you beat him again and again. You have pleasure from it. I see very plain what you are. A killer. I should not have brought you. My fault. Maybe the man will die . . . you hit him very hard."

"Broke his jaw, that's all. Maybe a couple of bones."

". . . Bad for him, bad for you, bad for the committee, for the men. It all go wrong. Maybe they will learn for next time."

My mouth was bleeding, my arms and shoulders were killing me, and he was preaching again. "Look at me!" I yelled, showing my bloodied mouth, the split gums. "The sonuvabitch was wearing knuckle dusters—aaa, what holy shit you dish out. The world stinks and you stink with it. You're no better'n I am . . . you beat your wife—"

"Watch what you say . . ."

"—then go after her with a gun. Good for her she had guts or you'd have killed her . . ."

"Keep quiet, kid."

I wasn't listening. It was too late now. That fucking machine—once it starts, it's so hard to stop. I screamed, "I bet you would! I bet!"

"KEEP A QUIET!"

"YOU KEEP A QUIET!"

"SHUT UP!"

"SHUT UP YOURSELF YOU GODDAMN DAGO BAS-TARD!"

He turned to face me and now there was killer written all over him, too. He knew it and I knew it. We were cut from one piece. The flivver was going eighty, rattling like a tin can on a carnival whip. He must have forgotten himself in his murderous anger, because he took his fisted hands off the wheel and raised them to whack me as we went around a curve.

"GRAB IT!"

Too late. The flivver careened off the road on two wheels, went tumbling down a bank, side over side, and I kept bouncing off the post until I came flying out as the door burst open.

When I opened my eyes, a couple of farmers were standing over me. The world seemed to be standing still. Birds immobile in mid-air. I shook my head—stretched my eyes wide—wondered what I was doing there.

One of the farmers asked me if I was all right. I nodded, blinked my eyes. No pain. There was a strange odor and I sniffed at it. Then I saw several curls of black smoke spiralling upward. The flivver! It was on fire—our stuff strewn all over the place.

I sat up. "ANGELO! WHERE'S ANGELO?"

They had pulled him out and had him under a blanket. I crawled to my knees, stood on my wobbly legs and ran to him, not feeling a thing. He was alive, gasping. They had covered his face with car grease for the burns. His eyes were closed, his great chest heaving, his face a blob of raw greased meat. The smell was sickening. I retched, controlled myself, fell to my knees near him. I couldn't say a word— just rocked back and forth, back and forth. The farmers stood around quietly, though one did say they had sent for an ambulance.

I kept looking at Angelo who smelled of burned flesh and black car grease. His breathing was a rasp, harsh, abrasive. I rocked back and forth, half in shock, mute.

A farmer nudged me. "Yer pa's tryin' tuh say somethin' to yuh, boy."

I focused on Angelo's burned face, and his eyes were open, fixing me with a stare. The pain was obviously excruciating. I leaned over and kissed his forehead, then began to cry.

Angelo closed his eyes, opened them, formed his lips to speak, as the ambulance siren was heard. "Don't talk, Angie, just rest. The doctor'll be here soon."

He kept his eyes fixed on me and all I could do was rock back and forth and cry.

After a pause, he whispered, "You understand?"

"Yeah, Angie . . ."

"You will remember?"

"I'll try . . ."

He closed his eyes and died.

He was buried in a small country cemetery, very plain. Some tombstones were very old, some very new. It was a sunny day cooled by a slight autumnal breeze. Louie and Ida Sica were there, Carmina in mourning. Angelina was coming by train and told us to go ahead. Kovac, Murphy and Scotty were there, too.

Louie Sica said a few words before they threw dirt on the coffin; we talked quietly a little while, then they all left.

The cemetery was empty of life except for me. I stood looking down on the bare grave. Then I fell to my knees and half lying on the mound I cried. At last controlling my grief I knelt and with five fingers plowed five furrows. I withdrew a fistful of wheat seed from my pocket and planted them in the neutral sod. Wheat for Angelo's earth.

I stood, withdrew another fistful of seed which I peppered around the bare mound. Wheat for the living creatures. A few kernels stuck to my moist hand. I sucked them into my mouth and slowly chewed the sweet grain.

Before passing through the cemetery gate, I looked back and saw several sparrows nipping at the seed around the grave, and I smiled sadly. As I ambled down the dirt road, it was the sweet taste of wheat mingled with the sadness which kept me upright.

Late afternoon the next day, the wind blowing, my mackinaw collar up against the gusty breeze, neat and clean, I walked down an old winding four-laner. More than halfway home, I stopped before a road sign: New York 220 miles.

I heard a car approaching and turned to thumb a ride. I wore a sad smile; the anger and the bitterness were gone. I was lonesome, maybe a little numb.

It took me a long time to stop looking around to see where Angelo Ferrara was. Now, suddenly, in my old age, he's with me again. And I keep hearing myself say, "It's hard, you old bastard—it's very hard."

NINA—1

Dear Mom & Dad,

Hello! So this is the famous Fairfield School!

Everything is pretty good so far. My room is slowly becoming less like a hospital and more like a home. Mom, I would like Eli's water color of you sitting on the rocker, my flag, and a few other things like flower pots, etc. I'll most likely be sending you items to add to the "bring up" list in my next letters.

My roommates are nice. Barbara, the one that came in while you were here is really nice, and I can see a close friendship blossoming with her. The other, Alice, is okay but very young and the type who is shocked at swear words, and nervous of talk of "good-looking guys" so I'll have more difficulty being her friend. She feels uncomfortable with me and Barb because we seem "so old" to her, so we introduced her to two other girls more or less like her and hopefully she'll stop feeling so terrified. She was really homesick the other night and was near tears which started me thinking of you and home so I quickly shut her up with "the beginning is always the worst" and "you'll meet millions" and finally we brought her down to our house mother who is really wonderful.

I've met lots of girls, most of which are nice. One, Louise, who lives across from Carol the other girl from Highview, is really nice, although she's a better friend to Louise than to me. They're very similar so I expect them to become either fast friends or bitter enemies within days. Carol is the girl I once told you and Dad about, you know, her bragging about sex, and I told her what Dad said, the chickens do it, dogs do it, even people do it, so what's there to brag about. She began to cry and then I felt sorry I said anything.

My schedule was all messed up—they gave me intensified Latin (of all things) instead of World Civilization, but Mr. Griggs is straightening it out for me. I've got regular French III this fall, Camus in winter and French drama in the spring. And I've got Geometry, Biology (advanced no less! I wonder how I managed that one), English and regular Art all year plus pottery in the spring. One bad thing is the only class I have any friends in is English, with Louise. All others I have "alone" plus lunch "alone." Oh, well, I guess that will make me meet even more people. We went into town this morning and I bought an extension cord (I've got one outlet and three plugs to plug in) and a bag of apples. Oh by the way, the food is all right. I eat much less though because it's too much of a pain to get seconds once the main dishes are finished by the initial serving of the table. Sunday we had turkey. Tonight ham. I've stayed away from gravies, Mom, don't worry. Breakfast and lunch are cafeteria style—stuff like dry cereal and/or pancakes, and soup and grilled cheese (or so they say—I myself couldn't find the cheese). The soup was good though (with a tablespoon of salt, of course). But I'm rarely ever hungry. Anyhow I've got my apples. I deposited the check and budgetted myself to $7 a week. I hope I'll survive.

Hockey practice was okay—but very tiring. I've heard the drama teacher is new and exciting, but as yet I haven't met him. VERY HANDSOME! I can't wait to start *that*.

The only time I've felt really lousy about being here was this morning, waking up. I'd dreamed all night of very normal home things—eating lunch in our kitchen,

trying on skirts of Molly's at her house—very realistic
dreams. And waking up to these white walls really sort of
scared me. But I started to read immediately and everyone was soon up and talking and the loneliness left. If
there is anything worse than loneliness I don't know what
it is. I guess mornings will always be the worst part of
the day.

But overall, Mom & Pops, I'm happy. Write or call soon,
and send me various addresses of people. I wrote a note
to Nanny Ruth, but I guess she'll never answer. Also to
Eli and Pete, who believe it or not sent me a letter—a
fairy tale about the family—the Aging Bull, the Great Pacifier, the Prophet Eli, and Judith (who cut Holofernes'
head off—do I come off like that?). He calls himself Diogenes. I wrote back and told him he was an Asshole. I
sent it to that smelly basement of his. Does he still live
there?

I hope you and the house and my sweet little cat Davey
are well. I sure miss her.

Mom, I assume you will send my letters on to Pops
when he goes out of town, so I don't have to write two
letters.

Love always,
Nina xxxxxooooxxxxx

P.S. Oh, yeah, thanks, Mom, for the stationery with my
very own name on top. And don't worry, Pops, I'll get
good marks and *keep* my scholarship next year, too.

Neen

OSSO BUCO AT THE
GRAN TICINO

Eli Miller was bragging.

He could always brag to Kathy Dubin because they'd been friends and lovers since the age of thirteen-and-a-half. Kathy and he were eating *osso buco* at the Gran Ticino restaurant on Thompson Street in Greenwich Village. The restaurant was one his parents went to when they were low on funds and wanted to eat out in New York. It had a terrazzo floor, mirrored walls in a beautifully proportioned room, was cheap, and the *osso buco* was great. Especially the sight of Kathy sucking the bone.

Outside it was raining hard and people were running madly for cover, yet the sun was shining and steam was rising from the asphalt. Inside it was pleasantly cool because of the ceiling fans and the tiled floor, and the diners kept their constant chatter at a murmur as the elderly Italian waiters leisurely served their trade.

Kathy and Eli sat at a table for two against the wall, under a mirror, sucking the sweet meat and marrow from the huge bones and sipping strong Italian red from their glasses. Kathy's long green eyes were intent on Eli as he spoke because she sensed that what he was saying was only tangentially related to what he meant. Eli had been a passionate young lover and was now a passionate old friend. The fact was, everything Eli did was done passionately—his loving, his hating, his painting, even his cleanliness. Eli showered thrice daily, once before he stood at his easel, the second after he finished working for the day, and the third before he went to sleep. He was a very clean young man; a little crazy, she thought, but she loved him, even though she now loved Jimmy Kelton and no longer slept with Eli Miller.

Eli never stopped keeping in touch with Kathy nor she with him. They had parted as lovers amicably because he had insisted they talk it out, try to understand each other's motives, even though he'd been hurt because she had begun to go out with another man. (She had been content to see both, but Eli had refused to go along with it; he would not have minded, he admitted, if it had been the other way round.) Their love affair up to that point had been monogamous, she never once wanting it any other way, he with strain, but with some deep inner compulsion to remain true to her. When they broke up his father and her mother were terribly upset, which, of course, was another story.

Eli was not only the cleanest man in Manhattan, he was also the tidiest, a young man who could not abide untidy quarters, untidy relationships, a chaotic world. Kathy thought it was almost as if he unconsciously recognized that if once he permitted disorder into his life he would never be capable of putting it in order again. He was perhaps overly cautious. Never tried to steal second base, which his younger brother Pete always tried to do. Nina, his kid sister, not only tried to steal second base, but third as well. Kathy couldn't help wonder what it was that made every Miller child so different, except perhaps because Max and Rebecca Miller were so totally different. At times, as Kathy well knew, Eli, as if in rebellion against his inner need for order and caution, would unaccountably let go. Attempt the immeasurably more hazardous steal of home plate. Insist that the peace demonstration be orderly and peaceful, and then be the first to provoke violence if a cop or bystander became what he thought was too obnoxious. It caught people by surprise. One moment they'd be sneering at what a careful kid he was, and the next exclaiming at what a nut. She couldn't help loving Eli—never forgetting Jimmy, of course—for his unaccountability. Eli came to understand and enjoy what he called this peculiarity in himself. It brought him to the attention of others. He was pleased when Kathy told him, when they first sat down, that she'd seen his picture in the morning papers a week or so ago.

"Everyone's going to think you're gay, Eli."

"You know I'm not."

"What about Becky and Max?"

"They also know I'm not."

"What about everyone else in the world?"

"Up theirs. If I were gay, I wouldn't conceal it."

Kathy smiled, her freckled face dimpling, her long green eyes narrowing and slanting upwards at their corners, so that Eli couldn't help but remark to himself that she resembled Botticelli's *Spring*. Her face revealed a fresh innocent cunning as if already at her early age she could decipher mysteries beyond even the wisdom of the Sphinx. Of course, she had an advantage the Sphinx never enjoyed, she was a doctoral student in Clinical Psychology.

"You love the idea of your friends all talking about you, wondering about you—is Eli Miller gay? It'll keep everyone up an extra hour at least, thinking about Eli Miller. You're still trying to impress Mummy and Daddy, aren't you?"

Eli's laugh was forced, and Kathy knew something was bothering Eli; she also knew that before the evening was out she would know what it was. "It's good we split up," he now said, "because life with you would be impossible. I went to the Gay demonstration because I sincerely believe Gays are treated unjustly and need the support of straights. I got myself clobbered by a cop because I lost my temper when a bystander said something nasty to me and I took a poke at him. There are a million ways a person can gain attention if—"

"And you know all of them," she said, then laughed again, as did he.

Sometimes, Kathy thought, they were like an old married couple who still loved each other, were completely at ease with each other. She wondered if it would ever be that way with Jimmy Kelton. Gave up wondering, and busied herself, as did Eli, sucking out the last of the marrow from her bone, having long before scavenged the last morsel of meat. Simultaneously, they laid their bones on the plate and raised their napkins to wipe mouths and hands. Then, again simultaneously, they raised their wine glasses and sipped. Eli's forehead was wrinkled with thought as Kathy peered at him.

To distract him, she asked, "What's happening with Pete and Nina these days?"

"There's something that's been bothering me for a couple of weeks. Upset my equilibrium. My pictures are off-balance, don't hold at the center—aah, to hell with it." He stared into space.

She saw that his eyes were troubled, that he was beginning to breathe more quickly, his Roman nose which hugged his face flaring at the nostrils. Yes, Eli was unhappy about something. What could it be? It was he who wasn't holding the center; it was his equilibrium which was upset. Yet, he looked so damned alive. How easy it would be for her to fall passionately in love with him again. His eager intensity when they were younger had begun to frighten her—who needed to be so totally possessed during puberty? She'd only wanted to be loved, to have fun, to play house—not to build a house. He'd had only one terrible overwhelming desire—to put it in no matter when or where. Let me put it in, Kathy, please! And she had let him when she would have preferred not to. His desire had overcome her, his pure obsession for her thin little body, and she had loved him so, just him, Eli Miller. It had been too much for a young girl and she'd been very unhappy. Besides, she'd needed to discover what other young men were like. Jim was easygoing, laid back, as the expression went, yet no less ambitious and hardworking than Eli. So damned different.

But now, she realized, she could love Eli and be happy about it, and of course he had outgrown that obsessive need to put it in, as if that were everything in life. He could wait ten minutes at least. His obsession to put it in had become an obsession to put it on canvas. The obsessed artist—who needed that?

But what was she thinking of? She loved Jim; she was going to live with him as soon as they could find an adequate apartment, and that was that! Eli was such a decent man, though, and would be obsessive all his life. Also egocentric, almost narcissistic, could be very selfish, yet kind, generous, too. A good friend. When he really lets go—more accurate perhaps, when he really gets going, God help the universe. Big galactic bangs. He had the energy, the strength, and the sheer drive to work around the clock. Like Max Miller, muscular and quick-tempered. The terrible fights they, Eli and his father, would have when Eli was a young boy—they didn't care if the entire world heard them. The little strong-willed boy standing face to face and toe to toe with the bull of a man who wanted his son to be rational and nonviolent as they pelted each other with dirty words—what an example for the child. Rebecca, both rational and nonviolent, would stand between them, speaking quietly through their raised voices, the basso of the man, the piping breaking voice of the young boy. She would calm them down, then the man and the boy would smile at each other through the tears and embrace, the man hugging the boy tightly so as to impress his life on the boy's young bones. Oddly, her own father would react with sympathy for Eli, "That Max Miller's a maniac," and her mother for Max, "That kid Eli's so wild-tempered a man would have to be a saint to restrain himself."

Her mother was soft on Max Miller, had met him a long time ago when her own parents had taken her to live and work on an anarchist commune in Michigan. She, Kathy, often wondered if Max Miller and Dina Dumashkin had done it together and if perhaps they did what they shouldn't have—kept encouraging Eli and Kathy to stay together, even to marry—because each was now sorry he or she hadn't married the other. Very complicated. As her mother always said, "Life does not move in a straight line, Kathy." A further complication was that the more Dina kept pushing her daughter to love and marry Eli Miller, the more Kathy resisted it. Would she resist it less if her mother stopped urging her? Damn them, can't they ever learn to keep their hands off? Eli had echoed that plaint a hundred times, using words so obscene that they must have burned even Max Miller's scarred ears to a crisp. Dina and Max. Had they or had they not? She had once thought of asking her mother but had stopped herself at the last moment. Why was she so damned curious about that? What was there in it for her? Like all budding psychologists, she wanted to know the inner lives of everyone she encountered, including mothers, fathers, siblings, friends, enemies. It never stopped. Rebecca and Sid Dubin, too. The world was so small, at least their world. Her father had met Max in the trade union movement after the war and they'd been enemies. Sid Dubin had been an anarchist nearly all his life and Max a Stalinist, for a time. Both believers to their very souls. Then Max broke with his faith over some evil business. He came to Sid Dubin and said straight out—later her father said only Max Miller could have the guts to do it that way—"Listen, Dubin, I've been wrong and you've been right. I'd be proud to be your friend."

Her father brought Max home to dinner. Dina looked at Max and Max looked at Dina and did not say a word for five minutes. Her father had to say, "Hey, Miller, stop ogling my wife." And then they all laughed at how small the world was, at least their world. And when her parents went to Highview-on-Hudson to have dinner with the Millers, Rebecca and her father got to talking and soon discovered they had many friends in common in Springfield, Massachusetts, Rebecca's home town and where Sid Dubin had broken his hump, as he said it, trying to organize textile machine factory workers. So it had been a reunion of sorts, and a great friendship was born. Sid Dubin became a high echelon leader in the union and Max Miller was one of his best organizers. "I don't want power, Dubin, that's for you, an old anarchist. Stalinism beat the desire for power out of me. I'm satisfied to be just an honest porkchopper. The wheel turns."

And when she was thirteen years old, a woman for not quite a year, she and Eli fell madly in love at the summer camp their parents had started for themselves and friends. They'd had so many happy years together—an enlarged family. Though recently when she'd come home from graduate school with Jimmy who was getting his doctorate this year, her father told them all at the dinner table that Max Miller was in a bad way, moody, always appeared to be tuned in elsewhere, driving the other organizers under him so harshly they had petitioned him to get Max off their backs. Would Eli be the same as his father when he got older?

She wondered now if what was troubling Eli was related to what was troubling his father. If she wanted, she could pry it out of him, but that would be unfair. All of them had been brought up never to be unfair. It was a burden they carried and she often thought that that very injunction was itself unfair. She observed the intense concentration with which Eli was molding a sculpture from the soft doughy centers of Italian bread. His fingers worked swiftly, expertly, his dark eyes slitted, the red point of his tongue extruding from one corner his mouth. She watched him, unaware that a soft smile further enhanced the innocent cunning of her lovely face.

At last, with a final little pat, he said, "That's it." He set it down on the table facing her. It was a grinning satyr about four inches high.

It was a lascivious little thing, and she laughed. He did not join her—his face was very serious. "I suppose you're telling me something," she said.

"Yes, I'm telling you something."

"I don't get it."

"Your new boy friend is dulling your wits," he said, looking her straight in the eye.

She challenged him, green eyes to ebony, then he turned his head to order espresso for both of them.

"Are you going to explain?"

"No, dammit, no! You should understand yourself."

"Screw you, Eli Miller!"

"Anytime you say, Red."

The waiter brought the espresso, and as they were both intently squeezing lemon rind, Eli said, "I must have drawn your picture a thousand times, and half the time it came out looking like a Titian nude—even though you're so skinny I wonder what your Jimmy sees in you—and the other half you look like my mother. Perhaps you can psychoanalyze that to death, too."

"Now you're getting nasty. I knew I shouldn't have come. But to put your mind at rest, Jimmy and I are looking for an apartment. It's over between you and me, try to remember that. But we'll be friends as long as we live, no matter how nasty you become."

"Forgive me," he said.

"Yes, for the one thousandth time."

Eli laughed, she as well. The espresso finished, the bill paid, they rose to leave the Gran Ticino.

Out in the crowded wet street, the day still lingered into the evening as if hanging on to the city's haze; they turned towards Washington Square Park. Eli took her hand in his and squeezed her fingers. She returned the squeeze—they'd been squeezing fingers since they were children, and she felt no twinge of guilt with regard to Jimmy. When they entered the park square he stopped dramatically in the middle of a stride, and said, "Do you want to come up to my cave and listen to music or look at my new drawings or what?"

She gazed at him with a mock smile. "What have you got on your mind?"

He laughed. "Not that—even though it would make our parents happy. But I want to show you some new drawings—doodles almost. I think they are the beginning of a new phase for me and I want your reaction to them—you always tell me the truth."

Kathy saw that he was serious, that it was very important to him. For some unaccountable reason, she had a feeling that they were both crazy, like a divorced couple who can never let go of each other, but she took his arm and followed him crosstown east.

Eli silently observed Kathy examining his drawings as they lay strewn over the white porcelain kitchen table under the strong white light. They were in Eli's fourth floor walk-up on East 15th Street, across the street from Stuyvesant High School. By strange coincidence, Max had lived in this same tenement with his mother and siblings some forty years before.

There was little change. The cockroaches, a phalanx of helmetted Roman soldiers, were retreating across the plains of the sink to hide in the walls. The white light seemed to frighten them, and many broke ranks and began to run, armor shining, Roman discipline in disarray.

Kathy, her red hair glistening under the white light, lifted one drawing, looked at it intently, put it down, returned to an earlier one, examined it, laid it on the table, lifted another she hadn't seen.

Eli eyed her impatiently. He had brought her to the apartment to tell him what she thought of them, why didn't she say something? All she had to do was say whether she liked them or not—he didn't need a critique, after all she wasn't an expert. Did she or didn't she like them, that was all he wanted to know.

Kathy didn't say a word. Merely kept turning from one drawing to another, backtracking, going further. Her full lips were pursed, her freckled forehead wrinkled, her long green eyes seriously at work.

He'd be damned if he would say anything. She would have to speak first, say exactly what she thought or he'd throttle her. It served him right, he shouldn't have shown them to her. He didn't have the slightest idea why he'd asked her up after they'd eaten. She really thought he was using that old device to get her up here so they could get laid. Nonsense. Oh, what's the difference whether she liked them or not—it was he who had to like them, they were his, and it was he who had to decide in the end whether they were any good.

Kathy didn't utter a sound. Her face showed nothing. Her green eyes examined, reflected, scrutinized, this way, that. It was almost as if, knowing he was impatient for her words, she had decided to make him wait. He had placed her in this position, she hadn't asked, so let him stew.

Eli sat on the corner of the table, his arms akimbo, his teeth clenched, his eyes glaring at her. He caught a glimpse of each drawing as she raised it to examine under the light and knew immediately every line, every problem it had presented, and exactly in what sequence it had been drawn. He had told her they were doodles. Doodles, my ass. Each had taken hours to draw—imagination, intelligence, craft, technique in constant conscious attendance. An idea, first hardly discernible, revealed its vague self, then burgeoned rapidly like proliferating amoebae, and he'd had to work fast before it got away from him. Ink figures. The lines uneasy, not sharp—uneasy to create unease, tension in a grotesque scene. Several succeeded, many half-failed, many more totally failed. The wastepaper basket overflowed. The half-failed he had decided to revisit, to study, to discover the one way to make them succeed. They were his, no one else's. He had not borrowed—to borrow implies an obligation to return—but had stolen to keep for himself. Stolen from Goya and even from a lesser artist like George Grosz and they would never get anything back from him. They were his. Only his. He had done them after that bizarre episode involving his mother—my God, how sickening, his own mother, how could she? Forget it. Just forget it! They had made him sick with unease, to look at them was to retch; he couldn't endure them a moment longer. How could he draw and paint when it was something he only felt but knew nothing about? To hell with it. . . . He didn't want to be brilliant, he wanted to be profound. Graduate school was a lark, too easy, the professors, most of them, too soft, too forgiving of their students, afraid of being disliked. He would give his eyeteeth for an old master painter who worked him to death. Yet, honestly, he knew that if any professor had been too harsh, too demanding, he would have rebelled. Ah, they were all lost in some zany maze with too many open gates leading to other open gates . . .

Kathy had laid down the last drawing and was peering at him with serious eyes. She was almost as tall as he so their eyes were just about level with one another's. What a wise, beautiful face she had, damn her. He said nothing, waited for her to speak. He realized it was very important to him what she thought, what she said. If anyone in the entire world knew him, it was Kathy. There was nothing he had kept from her for almost half his life. They were only in their early twenties and seemed to have been married a lifetime. Nothing but truth had ever divided them or pulled them together. He was suddenly jealous of any boy or man who had ever touched her, seen her naked, talked with her as he had. Her every line, frown, or smile were as known to him as his own. All he had to do was put his hand on her and she would not recoil, repel him. It would be like her own hand. There was a certainty of knowledge and understanding between them, not a scintilla of fear. A full knowledge. Yet mystery, too. He wanted to know every thought, every emotion with which she lived.

Suddenly she smiled at him, her long eyes crinkling at the edges, and he bathed in their warmth. Abruptly he knew what she would say about his drawings, and it would be to the point, accurate.

"They are marvelous, they are horrible," she said quietly. "They make me afraid. They are full of confusion and doubt. Some tell too much, don't conceal enough. Others not enough. Look at this one," she said, raising one that almost made him draw back in distaste. It was a very thin-lined drawing of half boy, half old hag, single breast on the thin body, a deflated breast, flat, decayed, the bony feet splayed, all lines tenuous, there and yet not there, and despite that solidly present. "It's as if your stomach were slit open and all your insides are hanging bare. How can you live that way, with all the pain showing, the disgust?" It was exactly the drawing that had made him throw pen to floor and run.

"Don't talk about me—just about them."

"But they are you," Kathy said, long green eyes slitted as they peered at him. "You've drawn yourself—revealed every pain, every horror inside yourself. It's like you've pulled a scab from a scar, begun to bleed, and then used your blood to draw."

"I said stop looking at them as if they're me, they are drawings consciously made, at least an attempt at art."

"They may be, I don't know, but they are you revealed— at least what you think of yourself. They are honest, but not telling the entire truth. You are lying, you are crying for yourself. It's right there, can't you see?"

"Stop being the shrink, Dr. Dubin. Are they good or are they bad?"

"Don't lose your temper or I'll slap your face."

"Sorry," he said.

"You mean the craft, the technique? Wonderful, marvelous, as far as I know anyway, and I don't know that much, do I?" Her face was grim now, almost angry. "You must yourself know whether they are good or bad, I don't have to tell you, you are your own worst critic—look at them and see."

Eli turned away, didn't want to see them—or her. The kitchen light was harsh. The drawings, the walls, the table, she, he himself, were unreal. Enlarged. Outsized.

Kathy went on. "It's like revealing one's personal diary entries—showing off only one's stink and decay. Is that what you think of yourself? of Rebecca—your own mother? Of me?"

"Leave Rebecca out of it, please."

"Yes. You're right. Why did you want me to see them? Why?"

He was adamant. "Why are you bringing it down to the subjective level—being the analyst again? They're drawings—not me."

"Because they're subjective, confessional, that's why. You are telling me something, yet also concealing something. Why?"

"What am I hiding?"

"Beauty," she murmured, "just beauty."

Eli turned to look at her familiar, lovely face. It was

sorrowful now, sad, her long eyes filled with tenderness. He wanted to lay his head on her breast, to feel her wonderfully familiar arms around him. He was frightened, and he needed her to console him, to reassure him, to whisper soft words in his ear as he had done many times for her. "Don't you understand?" he cried. "I need someone to see me, to know me. I feel so small and the world seems so large. I envy Pete his freedom, his ability to go out there to see, to sop it in, not to seem to give a damn how he is going to live his life. How am I going to live mine? What am I going to do? For an entire lifetime? It's cruel out there. So many you believe to be good turn out to be evil. Everyone seems armed with a machete, hacking their way through the underbrush. I'm scared, plain scared."

Kathy lowered her eyes, sighed. "So am I, Eli."

"Not as much as me. You were never scared as much as me."

She smiled at him, and they again peered into each other's eyes. "You're trying to make me into Becky again, but I'm not Becky, I'm Kathy Dubin. Remember?"

"You are a lot like Becky, everyone says so."

"Yes, good, solid Kathy. A sure thing. A pushover for tears. No, goddammit, I won't marry you, I won't be your —" Stopped in midsentence by the startled look on his face.

Then Eli began to laugh, standing close to her near the kitchen table, the white light harsh on their faces. She could feel the risibility start up in her chest, but made an effort to suppress it—if she laughed it would be fatal. But he was standing close to her, laughing now uncontrollably, the tears running down his cheeks, and then she began to laugh, too, her shoulders shaking, her breasts bobbing against his chest, and still Eli laughed, his face wet with tears, tongue tasting them at the corners of his mouth, stepping a few inches closer to her, so that her breasts now pressed hard against him. And she laughed, too, now the tears rolling down her cheeks, their eyes never once retreating, black and green glazed with tears, and she stepped a few inches closer to him, so that now her breasts were crushed against him, their stomachs touching, their hips pressing closer, their hands clenched at their sides.

The kitchen light was hot on their faces, and they saw one another large, outsized, every familiar blemish glistening from the tears and the white light, the drawings strewn about haphazardly on the table.

They laughed and laughed, the tears falling, their bodies crushed so close that they were almost one.

NINA—2

Dear Mom & Dad,

Just a short quick note to tell you I'm okay and in the full swing of things.

There are some people here I'd love you to meet. They're such characters, you know? It's incredible. I sat at a dinner table with one teacher named Mr. Stone, and also with Mr. Pritchett (my English teacher). First of all, Mr. Pritchett is something in himself. He looks just wild. Tall, flaring bulging dark eyes, little hair—mostly red, shiny baldness—but not like Tom Morrison in Highview. Much wilder sort of, like if he had hair it would be in complete disarray. He always has huge marks of sweat circling his underarms that stretch almost to his chest. Anyhow, he's very intelligent and not really radical, just intelligent and common sensical. Well, Mr. Stone is about as different as you can get. He looks exactly like the kid who graduated from a preppie prep school like Deerfield or something. But he's *super* insecure, oldfashioned and like a man reaching "old age" while he's really only in his thirties. He's a slight man but eats like anything. There was a constant under-the-breath contest going on between him and Mr. Pritchett about food.

(Waiter walks by with a tray of veal cutlets that resemble flattened fried turds.)

Nina laughs at the scene. Other Student moans and says: Not good ole deleesheeous veal cutlets *again* . . .

Mr. Pritchett (angrily buttering a roll): Jesus Christ, it's a wonder these kids live at all. What the hell do they *eat* anyway? (This is said more to himself than to anyone else—he half smiles saying it.)

(Mr. Pritchett and Nina catch eyes and laugh hopelessly.)

Mr. Stone (we've received our own tray of turds and he's begun to slap one down on each plate and pass it angrily to a student who looks very stoney himself): You know there's all too much complaining about the food in this school. (He's really muttering to himself.)

Mr. Pritchett (looking sort of surprised): Oh yeah?

Mr. Stone: Yes, well, you know, what do people expect? This is incredibly good institutional fare!!!

Mr. Pritchett: Oh yeah?

Mr. Stone (quieter now): Well, you know, people go on and on and *on* and it gets, well, it gets annoying, YOU KNOW?!

Mr. Pritchett: Well, it seems to me that lady (meaning the dietician) runs the place. No one goes near her. (Laughs a bit—ventures a taste of his turd.) God! (Gets up and leaves table to talk to a student sitting at nearby table.)

Mr. Stone: Just too much complaining . . . s'food . . . not bad. (He proceeds to get three gross looking turds while students force themselves to eat a few peas.)

———

Anyhow I could go on and on. *But* I'm missing lunch, so off I go to paradise!

Write again soon.

Love always,
Nina xxxxxxx

TO MA, WITH LOVE

Ruth Elias, a soft round little woman, sat sunk in upon herself in her wheelchair, her eyes closed against the morning sun.

Across the solarium floor and to the side, ancient but still beautiful Sarah stared into space, violently rubbing her puckered chin, endlessly repeating, "What have I got here?" despite the fact the nurse had shaved her chin that morning. Sarah was idiotically vain and drove the attendants batty everytime a hair appeared on her septuagenarian face or body.

Louis Friedman, aged ninety-six, his face pink with health, his noble nose a polished tusk, slumped in his customary place, skullcap on head, the fringe of his prayer shawl twined about his bony fingers, intoning from his prayer book. The chair next to his was empty, and no one dared sit in it because he guarded it for his wife now away in the hospital two weeks already and probably never to return to the old-age home. One of the old ladies had said bitterly, "His wife, what sort of wife? I'm as much his wife as she is. Here we are all his wives." Louis never listened to anyone. He prayed and guarded his wife's place.

Not far from Louis, sitting primly in a straightbacked chair, was Marian Ross, the old school teacher. She stared at, and probably through, the praying Louis. "There are some heads," she said in a clear and elegant diction, "that will always try to get the best of you. I never did trust them. I've never understood what it was to be kosher." She said it to no one in particular, and no one heard her, except Ruth, who smiled to herself. Marian carried on conversations with herself constantly.

Nearby two fat bulbous-nosed old women exchanged lies about their children and grandchildren. Underneath one, Sally Berman, a yellow puddle glistened. The other, Fanny Golan, sat with her heavy thighs spread wide and her skirt hiked up far above her knees. She rouged her face, her lipstick was brilliant, and she manicured her nails. Underneath her curled gray-brown wig her head was bald. Not because of religious scruples, but simply because she had lost all her hair at the age of seventy-five.

Not far from Sally and Fanny, in an easy chair in front of the TV lighted up with Sesame Street, lolled Izzy Smith, eighty-four, lean, mottle-skinned, and bald as well. He wasn't watching the children's program, but was turning constantly about, obviously worried by some terrible inner turmoil.

Alongside Ruth Elias, at a card table sewing a purse of simulated tapestry cloth by hand, bent Ben Stein, deaf but not mute though very silent. He was making the purse for Ruth, though it was supposed to be a secret. Ben was eighty-two, a strong little man whose forearm muscles expanded and contracted under the gray curly-haired skin as he plunged the thick needle in and out of the cloth. A porter, a slender middle-aged man who did his work very seriously, was mopping down the maroon linoleum floor.

Izzy Smith finally caught the porter's eye and with great urgency asked, "Well, what time is it?" The porter very patiently looked up at the clock on the wall directly in front of Izzy and said, "Eleven." Izzy smiled, calmed down, and moved his chair closer to the sun-drenched window. Again Ruth smiled to herself. Every morning was identical to every other morning. Now the porter would be near Sally and her puddle and Fanny with her hiked-up skirt and her spread thighs. Ruth cocked an ear the better to hear over Sesame Street, which no one ever watched but which was always on, some attendant's little joke. Now Ruth heard the porter's tired voice. "Sally, why don't you ask a nurse before and she'll take you to the bathroom?" Sally interrupted her anecdote about her favorite grandchild to ask, "How do you know it's mine?" "Sally, I've told you I can tell, it smells like yours."

Ruth laughed to herself, that would keep Sally quiet for at least five minutes. She opened her eyes and watched the porter mop up the puddle under Sally's chair. The porter could hardly avert his eyes from Fanny's grand opening, but because he was a kindly man, as quietly and as innocently as he could, he raised a work-worn hand and lowered her skirt to below her knees, then resumed his mopping.

Satisfied the morning drama was at an end, Ruth closed her eyes again, felt the warm sun on her cheeks, relaxed into her plumpness, and allowed herself to doze.

Ben Stein continued to sew the purse. Only recently he had learned this trade but already he possessed a good working skill. Not as fine as his skill with tin, after all he'd been a tinsmith for sixty years, and there wasn't a roof in Springfield on which he and his sons hadn't fitted gutters and flashing—*fleshing* to him—and leaders. In the old days Stein's revolving galvanized chimney caps—made in the shop by hand, his hands—had glistened over the city. Silent, efficient, responsive to the slightest breeze. No rain in your chimney, Mister, it will last—he said it *lest*—you ten years.

He had worked in shop and on roof into his seventies. His wife, Yetta, may she rest in peace, good riddance, had nagged at him to stop. "I'll stop when I know I can't do it anymore. I don't want to croak any more than you. I like it on the roof. I can see the whole city. All my chimneys, all my years on the roofs of Springfield, Mass." Ben was a man stubbornly proud of his work. His sons had wanted him to stop, too. Ashamed of what people might say about them, letting their old man climb long ladders and work on steep slippery roofs in the lousiest weather. But they had not continued to bother him about it long; they understood him, were good boys, already in their fifties themselves. Never stepped on a ladder anymore themselves, good contracts, a building boom, why should they work so hard? It was a new time, and he was an *alter hundt*, an old dog, he did what he liked.

Now he liked doing things for Ruth Elias, knew her and her family for over fifty years, had even been a pallbearer at Reuben Elias's funeral. A crazy nut if ever there was one. Died all those years ago from a heart attack suffered while fornicating with the Roumanian widow, Mrs. Lupowitz. An extremely strong man, Reuben had dragged himself from her bed, and the police found him on the lawn. He died a few days later in his flat in that old triple-decker, leaving a wife and seven children. Poor, destitute, the recipients of charity. Reuben Elias had been the finest blacksmith in Springfield, a topnotch toolmaker, but had found it difficult to keep a job because he'd been a wild revolutionary and had fought with every foreman in every factory in central and western Massachusetts. Brought up his children to be Bolsheviks, too, all of them crazy, not Ruth, she was a wonderful woman. Still, all her children had grown up and seemed to be doing well. He liked them, but especially he liked Ruth. Enjoyed pushing her around in her wheelchair, trying to get her to walk before she forgot how altogether.

Ben had gone deaf in his early seventies but he could read lips—he was no dummy—though when Ruth talked he read both her lips and her eyes. Her eyes were expressive, and even in her saddest days a wry humor shone in them. He knew she was pleased with his attentions. It made him angry, though, at how agitated she became when Harry O'Neill, the attendant, entered the room. She certainly liked Harry. Harry, to be fair to him, smiled and passed on.

After her hip operation, when she returned to the old-age home from the hospital and could sit up but not leave her bed, when she had to go, Harry would pick her up in his arms—he was a *shtarker*, a strong man—and carry her to the toilet, raise her nightgown for her and set her down, then wait outside. Finished, she would knock on the door and Harry would again lift her in his arms and return her to the bed, smooth the blanket for her, smile, nod, and leave. "Why shouldn't I like Harry?" she said. "We've been very intimate. No man ever did anything like that for me before." Ruth laughed, her eyes twinkling. Ben would have been very happy to do the same for her. He was sure he still could, even though he was over eighty. But with him Ruth was very modest. She was a shy, reserved woman. Though he remembered there had been stories about her after Reuben died years ago. Shep Nielson, one of Reuben's young friends and comrades, a *goy*—aaa, what was he, Ben Stein, an angel?

Ben worked on the purse he was secretly making for Ruth. Ruth snored, not harshly, but shyly, reservedly, like Ruth herself. A quiet, timid little woman.

Sarah kept pulling at her puckered chin, asking, "What have I got here?" Old Louis Friedman was intoning his prayers and keeping an eye on the empty chair near him. Sally and Fanny had resumed where they'd left off—Fanny's thighs were outspread, but no new puddle as yet reflected light under Sally's chair. Izzy Smith had again become panicky, was biting his nails, his eyes wandering wildly, worrying about the time. "Brains are difficult to come by, I can tell you that," Miss Ross, the old school teacher, said to no one in particular.

Though invisible to the naked eye, the card table on which Ben Stein sewed began to quiver in a rhythmic pattern. He recognized the cause immediately—the telephone was ringing. He raised his head to see the young female attendant answer it. Her bored eyes searched and found Ruth Elias. Ben jumped from his chair and with a quiet tenderness shook Ruth's shoulder. She awoke, saw Ben, smiled sadly. What dream had he interrupted?

"The phone," he said in his low harsh voice.

She smiled. He wheeled her to the phone and then placed the instrument in her hands, turned and left her. Ruth was a private lady.

"Hello, hello."

"Hello, Ma."

"Polly?"

"No, Ma, this is Becky. How are you?"

"Oh . . . well."

"Oh well what?"

"I'm all right, I guess."

"Is there anything wrong?"

"I'm fine. It just hurts. How's Max, the children?"

"As far as I know they're all well. I'll probably come up to see you next week. Is there anything you want?"

"What do I want?" Even in Ruth's own ears it sounded like, "What don't I want?"

"Polly comes several times a week. So does Emanuel. Sophie writes you long letters a couple times a month, Mimi, too. I come frequently to visit, call you almost every other day . . ."

Ruth laughed. "I'm greedy. Do you have to remind me?"

Now Becky laughed, too. "Are you walking yet?"

"What do I need to walk for, I've got the deaf one to push me around. He loves to push." She laughed again.

"Push him back, Ma."

"I wish I could, what do you think?" Now they both laughed.

"Have you heard from Nina, Eli?"

"They write very often—they're good grandchildren, better than my own sons."

"You haven't heard from Jack then?"

"He means well, he's too busy, poor man. Your Nina tells me everything—doesn't leave out a thing—tells me things I don't even want to know. How could you let her go off to private school at her age? Not yet sixteen—a baby. I'm surprised Max let her go."

"She wanted to go. She got a scholarship. We let her go. Don't worry about her—though I must say I'm sorry now myself, but for me, not for her. You know, Ma, you were barely older than her when you left your parents and came to a strange land, perhaps never to see your mother and father again. Remember?

"Well, things were different then. We became grownups at ten, not forty like today."

"Don't worry about—"

"Everyone says don't worry. I don't worry, the pain in my hip is too much. I can't sleep, can't walk. I'm finished, Beck-eleh."

"The doctor said if you'd try to walk it would heal faster. Try it and see."

"Here comes Harry, such a nice man."

She could hear Rebecca giggling. "There's plenty of life in you still, Ma."

"You're keeping my apartment, paying the rent?"

"Of course." Ruth knew Rebecca was lying, but was glad she was. "By the way, do you mind if I take Shep's portrait of me? I'd like to have it."

"But of course you can take it, it's yours."

"Okay, Mom, see you next week I hope."

"Bring me a fresh chalah and a quarter pound of Philadelphia cream cheese. The food here is lousy. Give Max my regards."

"He sends his."

"Becky?"

"Yes?"

"Why do you sound so sad?"

"Me?"

"I am not deaf yet, I can hear very well. Is there something wrong between you and Max?"

"No!"

"I'm sorry, I shouldn't interfere in your life."

"You can interfere all you goddam please, you're my mother."

"This isn't like you, what's wrong?"

"I'm sorry, Ma. I don't have to tell you, you know yourself, and know it very well, when you have children, a husband, a life to live yourself, there's always something, always something . . ."

Ruth sighed. "Yes, yes, I know. And it's time you knew, my child, not even the Devil can stop the clock from ticking."

They were both silent for a moment.

"Be well, Becky."

"You, too, Ma."

After Ben Stein had pushed her out into the sun again, Ruth gazed into his tiny bright green eyes, into his bright monkeyface so he could read her lips, and said, "She's a fine woman, my Becky. The best. All my children are the best."

Yes, he nodded, of course.

"She's too good, that's all. Like I was. Too good to her husband, to her children. Everyone takes advantage of her. I told her a million times not to be so good, to fight back. I know from long experience. She laughs, never cries, not her. But sometimes I know she laughs with tears in her eyes."

"Yes," Ben whispered in his harsh voice, "we old ones laugh with tears in our eyes, too. Old heads, old bones, old tears. Eighty years old is pretty old."

Ruth wasn't listening. "Now she was laughing with tears in her eyes. She thinks I can't tell, I'm an old foolish woman."

Yes, Ben nodded, we are old and we are foolish.

"A woman's life is hard," Ruth said. "Very hard." Now she asked him, "When is breakfast?"

He smiled kindly at her. "It's lunchtime, they're bringing in the trays down the hall."

"Breakfast, lunch, it is all the same, I can't walk, but I can always eat," and she laughed.

With the help of Ben Stein's aged but still strong arms, Ruth made the difficult passage from wheelchair to stationary chair without too much fuss. She hated to make a fuss, she was a private woman, and it was bad enough she had to eat at a table with people she called strangers even though she'd been their companion now for five months and in fact had known several of them almost all her lifetime. For a minute she observed them. Blind Morris ate with an intense concentration—later he would exult at not having spilled a drop. Louis Friedman ate without even for a moment interrupting his dialogue with the Nameless One, the Holy of Holies, rocking his body back and forth in rhythm to the eternal words. Sarah was fed by the young female attendant because she refused to take the hand concealing the hairs that blemished her beauty from her chin. Weak-bladdered Sally picked at her food like a bird, her eyes ever alert for those who might rob her. Fat Fanny ate with her snout in the dish. Ben ate like a man accustomed to working with tools—they must do the job for which they were intended with precision and economy of movement. Little waste—neatly. It reminded her of Reuben, the most fastidious of men. A white shirt had to be boiled, starched, and ironed each day, so that after supper he could shave, dress, and leave for the evening. He went out, the tsar. Where? Don't nag. A free thinker, a fervent advocate of revolution, he treated his wife like a serf—an animal. As if she couldn't read. She could read better than he, Yiddish, English, and Russian, too. Now she didn't read. Her eyes hurt her, she was too tired, her mind wandered. "It covers the water-front," she told her son, Jack, when he remembered to phone.

Why didn't he call more often, what was wrong with him? He was a learned man, but he forgot to call his mother. She forgave him. "You always forgive him," her other children said, and they were right. Deep in her heart she confessed she loved him the most of her children. Why not? His life had been the most difficult, and he had complained the least. His father had been cruelest to him, and when his father had died, he worked, scrounged, slaved to support a large family until his eyes sank deep into his head, two burning coals. And late at night, after everyone was asleep, he would sit in the kitchen near the black coal stove and read and read. At six in the morning, black lunchpail in his hand, he would leave for work, a young boy. The war against that plague, that devil, that unspeakable one, sent him into the army—he asked for no deferment because of dependents (he said it was more important to fight Nazism, but in her heart she felt it was because it gave him an opportunity at last to get away from the family)—and after a few years managed to return home alive, a man, quiet, his eyes still burning deep in his head. Then he went off to college and came home rarely since. So he forgot to call, so what? But it hurt, and everytime she was called to the phone she prayed to God it was he. Poor man, a learned professor, divorced, children running wildly about the street . . .

Ruth ate all the food placed before her, today herring and boiled potatoes with sour cream, two slices of pumpernickel and butter, followed by two cups of coffee and a heaping bowl of fruit compote, good for the bowel movement.

Finished, she searched the eyes of the young skinny attendant who wore skirts so short her bellybutton showed.

"That's enough, Ruth," the skinny girl said. "You'll get indigestion again, remember?"

Yes, Ruth remembered. Unlike the others—not Ben Stein—she could remember from minute to minute—well, not quite, and not always—from day to day, month to month, year to year. Life to life. She wasn't senile—merely old. Seventy-seven. Eighty, to be truthful. So the citizenship papers said eighty-three, so what, a mistake. And she could see pretty good, could hear, remember, sleep, go to the bathroom, and eat like a horse. Just couldn't walk. The doctor, the nurses, attendants, Ben Stein, her children, everyone, the entire world, said if she made an effort she would soon be able to get around with a cane. Effort. Enough effort already. She was tired, couldn't they understand? Tired, that's all. She had Ben Stein to push her. And if his hand slipped occasionally, as it did, she didn't mind a touch. "It still feels good, believe it or not." She could say that to Polly and Becky and they would laugh. But not to her other children, they became easily embarrassed the way she used to. Mothers and fathers themselves and still they blushed when she said it, fidgetted—c¹d people are not supposed to feel. They'd be surprised, yes, surprised if they knew the dreams she had. For some reason she remembered now when she was a girl in Odessa, already menstruating, and thinking babies came from kissing. So why did it get so hot between the legs? She had learned. Her children must have learned, too. How many of their own did they already have? She loved to count them—like a miser his fortune—even though she would probably never see most of them again. They'd gone off just as she'd gone off never to see her grandparents and parents ever again. They had, some of her grandchildren, wives and husbands she'd never met. Several were already expecting so that soon she would have two or three great-grandchildren. She was about to add, if I live, but said instead, to the devil with that. Not that she didn't have long moments of self-pity for the years, but not right now when she was counting her treasures.

Ben had completed eating and again helped her, this time from the stationary to the wheelchair. And again, of course, stole a feel with his hand. She ignored him as he rolled her down the corridor to her room for the afternoon nap. She remembered suddenly something he had said years ago, when he was, at least in their circle, thought of as a rich man, with a good business, a private house, cars, and the like. He'd met her in the street and she'd complained about their plight. And Ben, in the arrogance of his wealth, had said, "Oh, Mrs. Elias, you're a rich woman, you have riches beyond money! Your children are your wealth, your treasure."

"Yes, such wealth," she'd responded. Who was this man, who didn't know what it was to go hungry, to tell her her children were her wealth? Could she eat them? Could they eat her?

But now it was true, her children were her wealth and she hoarded them like a miser. And with all his money, here he was in the old-age home, no different from her. A place permeated with the odor of urine and feces, of old age, like bed linen too long slept in before being given an airing. So as he pushed her down the long corridor, she counted her wealth.

Jack, the oldest, had three, teen-agers in a broken home. The years will go; maybe their wounds would heal to leave little not quite invisible scars.

Sophie had two, Reuben and Dorothea. Reuben was a Ph.D. and now his wife Alicia, too, Sophie had written. Sophie wrote the best letters—long, filled with details of her family's life, so that Ruth always knew what they were doing, accomplishing, and only good news, never bad. Dorothea was married, too, and perhaps would soon have a baby. If she forgot the pill. Oh, if only she'd had a pill. Who would she have given up? None. When you had them, you loved them. If not, well, what you don't have you don't miss.

Unless you have none, then you miss plenty. Two of her own had died in infancy. At the time a tragedy, now forgotten. Not quite—two little scars on her heart. Two scars among how many? Not now, not when she was counting her treasures. Three and two make five.

Polly had five, three girls, two boys. Polly loved to push, hot coals in her panties and a voice like an angel. In her house drums banged, the piano never stopped, guitars, singing. A noisy house. Her oldest, Jeanie, was married and pregnant. So how many was that? Five and five make ten. If Polly's children were like their mother they alone would make fifty. You can't count the baby in the belly, that's bad luck.

Mimi wrote, phoned, always sent money when it was needed, flew in from Oregon every couple of years, was a fine daughter. Had a marvelous husband and two beautiful daughters with hair as red as fire. Laura, the youngest, was pregnant already while going to college with her husband. Ten and two make twelve.

Emanuel, the silent one, the big-hearted one, had three, two girls and a boy—real students, smart as whips, still young. Twelve and three make fifteen.

And Leonard, her baby, her poor baby, what happened to him? Lives in one place, then another, she wouldn't hear from him for a year, then suddenly a phone call, "Mom, how are yuh, I'm gonna come see yuh. Fly in. How are yuh, Mom?" He came once in ten years. A gambler, separated, two girls, who knew anything about them? Fifteen and two make seventeen . . .

Ruth became frightened. There was something wrong. Seventeen wasn't quite right. Who had stolen her treasures? Whom did she forget?

Sweating, biting her lips, she began to concentrate, to count her children again, to rummage around in the thicket of her years. Oh, my God, Becky. Why did she always forget

Becky? She loved her as much as she loved the others, maybe more. Rebecca was the most generous of her children, had taken her into her own home for years, was patient and understanding and loving. She always forgot Becky. Why? It hurt Ruth, drove her to despair, it was something she didn't want to think about. Becky, my sweet child, forgive me, I love you deeply, honest, I do. Forget it, she said to herself, your life is coming to an end. . . . Becky and Max had three—that Nina was a flame, not yet sixteen and already off to school, they should put iron pants on her behind. Eli, Becky's oldest, was a fine young man who never forgot his grandmother, yet strange, wild. And Peter, a lonely, quiet, handsome boy, a runner who made jokes to conceal his sadness, born wise. . . . Seventeen and three make twenty.

Seven sons and daughters, twenty grandchildren, and soon, Ruth hoped, many great-grandchildren. Not bad for a life's work. Pretty good. Once before she left this world for the next she would love to see them all in one room—it would have to be a large room, daughters, sons, their husbands and wives, grandchildren with their wives and husbands, and great-grandchildren rolling and tumbling on the floor. No! What's the sense of dreaming? And yet why not? Was she too old to dream? She obtained her greatest pleasure from dreaming, and she'd earned every dream. When dreams stop, life stops.

When you sleep and dream, what comes comes, you can't control it, the good and the bad, the terrors, the fears, the happinesses, the pleasures, the nightmares, the aches and pains, but when you sit and dream, daydream, then you can dream what you want, like a god, chase off the bad dreams, immerse yourself in the good ones, play with them, nibble on them, give yourself a secret joy, keep them going endlessly, oblivious to the world, float on your dreams in your own self-made paradise, and if sometimes a sad one slips in, and it gives you a sweet agony, so you embrace it to your soft breast, you hold it tight and you weep sweet sad tears, for that can give pleasure, too, not the terrors, the fears, who wants them, who needs them, you can live without them, but the sweet sad agony, it adds to your life, to your dreams, oh, yes, yes . . .

'All right, Ben, stop pushing." Ruth laughed and Ben smiled. In helping her from the wheelchair to the bed, his hand had slipped again and felt her breast. Had himself a feel. The old rooster. Monkeyface.

Ruth gazed at him tenderly from her pillow. With him around the attendants and nurses didn't have any work to do—for her, anyway. Ben peered at her intensely, as if trying to read her mind. Little bright eyes in a monkeyface. Suddenly his hand reached over and softly caressed her cheek; she could feel his calluses, and her heart quickened and she touched his old hand with hers. Don't be bashful, she felt like saying, close the door and lie down, we'll hold each other, it's not a sin anymore at our age, but she merely closed her eyes and she could hear him tiptoe from the room. He would sit in the solarium and work on the purse he was secretly making for her, but she knew, of course. Why did she need a purse? For what? Her gold? Her heart was her purse, and her children were accounted for and locked safely in. Ben was too shy. Reuben would have jumped in—what a jumper he had been in his day. He hadn't been afraid of man, woman, beast. An insane man, with a temper like a wild dog. Danced like a wild Cossack. A *vildeh chaiye*—a wild beast. Even as a boy.

They had lived on the same street in the ghetto of Odessa. A muddy street with tiny houses leaning into each other, holding each other up, just like the people who lived there, because in their hearts fear huddled, too. Who could tell when the *kulaks* and *muzhiks* inflamed with whiskey would come bellowing in, burning houses, beating the men, raping the women, even young girls. Or even the Cossacks, the soldiers of the tsar, the swine. But there were some who weren't afraid. When Reuben was fifteen years old all of Odessa knew him. Strong as an ox, he had almost killed a Ukrainian peasant for having accosted his sister Bella, may she rest in peace and Hitler fry in hell. They thought all Jewish women were whores, dying to sleep with them. For a year Reuben was concealed by his people, he even stayed in the dirt cellar of her father's house for a week, a short wide-shouldered boy with sprightly bright black eyes and a large head covered with snarled black curls. She could hear him laughing, singing, cursing, pacing back and forth like a caged beast. Then late one night he was gone to hide in another's house. When he emerged from hiding he was a revolutionary. He drove the Jews of Odessa crazy, afraid that his terrorism would bring disaster down on them—the drunken peasants, the Cossacks, the police. For the protection of Jews there were no laws—one could steal from them, kill them, rape them. We are few, they are many, they will decimate us, destroy us. God's greatest commandment is to live. That is not my commandment, Reuben said, mine is that it is better to die fighting than to live frightened. Our way, God's way, we have survived as a people for nineteen hundred years against the barbarians. My way there will be no barbarians. And our people shall all be dead.

Every day she would see Reuben Elias on their street, his hair black as pitch, never combed, wild, eyes like brilliant black diamonds. She loved him. All the girls loved him—and it was said he loved them all, too. One day she was a child, the next a woman, her bosoms round and hard as Ukrainian apples, the finest in the world. Her mouth watered at the remembrance of them. Her father said Reuben Elias was a courier for the Social Revolutionaries, also a bandit—not for himself, for the revolution. One day when she was coming home from the *mikvah*, the baths, a woman already two years, he stood before her, her heart pounded like the beat of hooves, and he smiled, his strong teeth large and white, his eyes bright and tender.

"Hello, Ruth," he said, her heart beat so quickly she thought she would faint. She blanched, she blushed, she didn't know what to do with her eyes, her hands. "In another year or so I will ask your father for your hand. You are already the most beautiful girl in Odessa." Then with great dignity, he was seventeen years old, he turned quietly, not wildly, and stalked away, his shoulders broad, square, his head a snarl of black curls. From that moment on, every time they met on the street, he would come to speak to her, to ask her how she was, her head bowed, her face flushed, her mouth speechless, and he would take her hand in his broad fist for a second, stroke it tenderly, and leave.

The tsar wanted men for his army and sent his police to take them. Many young men of the Odessa ghetto ran away. Fight for the tsar? Reuben ran all the way to Petersburg. Arrived in time to join a conspiracy to assassinate the tsar. The police learned of it and raided the cellar in which the conspirators met. Reuben escaped. Soon his parents heard he'd gone to America. Everyone mourned his going. A year later a letter came to Ruth's father. "I ask for your daughter Ruth's hand in marriage. I am working as a blacksmith and will soon have enough money to send for her." She told her father yes, even though her mother warned her, as she herself would some day warn her daughter Rebecca about Max, that Reuben Elias was a wild man who would never give her a moment's peace. A mother's heart knows even if her brain doesn't know why. (Her mother had been right, though she herself had been wrong about Max—at least for the most part.) So the Eliases and the Volodins exchanged smiles and kisses and wild blackberry wine. There was a party in the street, the mud dried from the sun, all relatives of both families and neighbors were present. They danced, they sang, they ate honey cake with raisins and nuts. She sat like a bride in a white dress to her ankles, not dancing with anyone, of course.

Time did not fly, it trudged. She and Reuben exchanged letters. He was working, he was saving, but things were difficult. Money did not grow on trees. It never does for the poor. For the rich, wherever they shit they find gold.

Though after the 1905 revolution a Duma had been formed and the serfs had been freed, for the Jews little had changed. The ignorant Ukrainian peasant with his vodka and his cruelty to make up for his own hard life—to him the Jew was a rabbit to be killed and flayed.

Ruth remembered a poem her father had taught her when she was a child. A Cossack mother sings her baby son to sleep: "I will buy you a horse, my child, and you will ride it to Odessa/There you will rob and beat the Jews and return to me with presents/And if I don't like them, you will return to Odessa to rob and beat the Jews again . . ."

Ruth sighed, stared out the window, pondered mothers and their sons, drifted back to the past, to Reuben . . . . She waited for him; she was his bride. A letter arrived, a package with a dress; she wore it day and night. Some of her older sisters had already gone to America. Friends. Entire families.

At long last, right before the outbreak of war in Europe, just when she had given up all hope, thought perhaps she ought to find another, the money arrived from Reuben. She danced and cried. Her father smiled sadly. Her mother wept. "I'll send for you, Mama, I promise." Her younger brother, Barash, clung to her skirts, hugged her, wouldn't let go. Arrangements were made. Until she and Reuben were married, she would stay in a town called Palmer with her sister Lilly who had married Samuel Boxer, another man from Odessa. She said good-bye to her father and mother, never to be seen again. Good-bye to her brother Barash, never to be seen again, may Hitler squirm in hell for eternity. Good-bye, good-bye, the tears flooded the streets of Odessa. The ship stank like an outhouse. There were many tears—but there was also hope. America . . .

Ruth sighed. The old bones ached. The tears never stopped. Aaa, why remember old pains? One loved for whatever reason, only God knew and He was a clumsy shoemaker, all thumbs. The truth was that among the tears there had been laughter and songs, especially when there had been a bite to eat for the children, for them. She and Reuben had been strangers in a strange land when they married and terribly young. Reuben pushed and pushed, she pushed back, so there were nine children, two died in infancy. Reuben raged against the world, against the capitalists, fought foremen, shouted invectives at his fellow workers, "Dirty cowards!" and she labored to rear her children and keep him in clean starched shirts so he could seek succor in the evenings with other women. They hungered, they suffered, and when Reuben died leaving her filled with hatred and shame, they were still hungry, still suffering, and probably till the last they were still strangers, too. By the time the last child left the house, Leonard, at the age of eighteen, there was finally enough to eat. And then? Just then old age began. Before she knew it, there it was. Old age—to the devil with it . . .

Little monkeyface was peeking into her room, and she beckoned him with her hand. His little bright eyes intent on her lips, she said, "Sit here while I nap, the attendants won't bother you." He smiled happily and sat on the chair near the foot of the bed.

Ruth closed her eyes and was soon fast asleep.

Ruth slept with her head on Shep Nielsen's bony white breast all afternoon, and when she awoke she could somehow feel his long hairless body in the bed with her, and could even remember his uncircumsized thing, long, thin, and white, too. When she had seen it for the first time, she had felt a terrible shame. He was a gentile, an enemy of her people. She had looked away, not touched it with her hand—not right away.

How different from Reuben he was—like a young boy, innocent, tender. He told her he loved her, but she didn't believe him. She believed he loved her daughter Sophie and knew he had asked her to marry him and been refused. So he came to Sophie's mother, his friend Reuben's widow; he was so alone, without family and friends of his own. He lived in a boarding house a few blocks away, where he painted and drew and read books. He worked in a bookstore downtown, where he earned a meager living. He did not need much because he ate very little, wore the same black trousers too short for his long legs, the same threadbare black jacket, its sleeves too short for his long arms, and never had his hair cut, his long ash blond hair silky around his ears. A quiet, tender man, he was a passionate believer in the revolution, an idealist. It was Reuben who had urged him to join the Party, and it was her daughter and son-in-law, Sophie and Abe, who had him expelled years later for saying that Stalin was a murderer. And Reuben who had driven him away . . . . Ruth sighed deeply, it was long ago, there was no sense in reviving the bitterness.

When there hadn't been enough food, Shep brought large brown paper bags of bread and rolls and vegetables and meat. When there had been enough, he brought a bottle of wine, cake, fruit, and spoke quietly and gently to the children, to her. He came twice every week in the afternoon, when the children were in school or working. They were lovers. She, Ruth Elias, had a lover—something she had never dreamed of. He treated her with respect, never shouted at her, listened to her when she spoke, brought her books to read, and then talked to her about them. With him she was a human being, not a rag as she'd been with Reuben whose children she bore, whose white shirts she had washed and ironed so he could run off to sleep with his whores. But she had loved Reuben. Why? Because. What had she felt for Shep? Love, too, of a sort. A quiet, gentle love. He had asked her to marry him so they would not have to hide what they were doing. But she couldn't do that, she was more than fourteen years older than he. She already had a married daughter by then, she still felt loyal to Reuben, what would the children say, the neighbors? The world would laugh at her. But he did move into the house later as a boarder. Now Ruth laughed. Whom did they fool? The children, of course, but only for a short time. They were lovers—the children loved him, too, that was enough.

Over the years she had often wondered why she had permitted him to move in, but now of course she knew, understood. Once a week for months Becky had been going to his boarding-house room from her job after school to sit for a painting, and Ruth had bitten her nails. All alone with her fifteen-year-old daughter, a beauty with young round breasts, and him with his long thin white thing in his trousers. If he didn't keep it to himself, she would kill him.

When Becky would come home she would question her, how did it go, and Becky would say it went fine. You're not posing naked? Oh, no, Mom, what's the matter with you? And what do you do while he paints? We talk, Mama. It's wonderful. He talks to me like I'm a grown-up, about philosophy and books and painting, or we listen to his phonograph. He is a wonderful man, Mom. Yes, her mother agreed, he is a wonderful man.

Of course, Shep had told her that Rebecca needed this special attention. For reasons unknown the child had been badly treated in the family. Reuben had been almost as cruel to her as to Jack, always shouted at her, slapped her, pinched her, called her a *schlumper*, a klutz. Once he had caught her sitting with a boy on the back steps and had almost killed the child. Whore! Slut! So that the entire neighborhood had heard and Becky had been ashamed to go into the street. And she, Ruth, too, had always been at the child, why, God knows—no, Ruth knows, but not now. Sad, unhappy because of her father's treatment of her, still Becky always sang songs—knew every folk song, workers' song, popular song—when she helped about the house, did her homework. Becky and Polly kept the house alive with their singing even when they were most miserable, Becky's voice soft and low, Polly's ringing. Unhappy, bittersweet, Becky had become very quiet, a good girl as she grew up, the most generous of her children—except when she wanted something badly, oh, she never stopped fighting until she got it. Becky had her ways, Shep had noticed and thought that the child would appreciate some quiet attention, and she, Ruth, had worried about what went on in his room those afternoons.

Once, when none of the other children were around, Rebecca said, Mom, you don't have to worry. Who says I'm worrying? You are, Mom, and you don't have to. He's never touched me. Do you want him to touch you? Oh, Mom!— He's an *old* man. Rebecca blushed, and so did she.

It was just a few years ago, when she was still living with Becky and her family, that her daughter said, looking her straight in the eye, Shep would have made a fine husband, Mom. And she, Ruth, blushed, still guilty, still ashamed, because she could see her daughter was telling her she knew. You knew, Beckeleh? . . . Yes. I don't know if the others knew, we never spoke about it, but I did. I came home one afternoon. . . . Oh, my God! Mom, for goodness sake, we're not children anymore. You had a right, you had every right in the world, it wasn't as if Pa were alive. Shep was one of the nicest men I've ever known. He deserved you and you deserved him. . . . You think I'm nice, Becky? You're the nicest lady in the whole world, Ma.

They had hugged and kissed, and, finally, she no longer felt ashamed about Shep.

They lived together for almost two years. He became thinner and thinner, and she asked him to go to a doctor, but he smiled, he didn't eat much, he was healthy. Then it was too late. TB. He died in the hospital. Sophie and Abe, those passionate humanitarians, wouldn't even go to his funeral, only she and the younger children. She had wept quietly in the night. During the day life must go on, but at night, alone, one can weep all one pleases.

Ruth wiped the tears from her eyes, groaned, sat up, heavily and clumsily moved her feet so they hung down from the side of the bed. She could hear the slow shuffle of old footsteps in the corridor, the sharp click of young heels. The traffic was heavy. Supper was being prepared—it must be getting close to four o'clock. The days passed quickly here. Too quickly. Where was Ben Stein? Very strange. She wondered if she might have insulted him in some way. Sometimes she did without even realizing it. She was becoming grumpy in her old age, sharp-tongued, making up for lost time. She hardly cared if people didn't love her. Now that she was an old woman in an old-age home she could afford to be independent.

She glanced at the wheelchair near the foot of the bed. If Ben didn't come she would have to get into it herself. Perhaps she better ring the bell and Harry, the attendant, would come. He would pick her up in his strong arms and carry her to the chair. She still liked strong arms, they felt wonderful around her body. Stop the nonsense, where's Ben? This was unlike him. He had been at her beck and call for weeks without her even having to say a word or give him a look.

Ruth measured the distance to the wheelchair with her eyes. She had better hurry; she could hear the clatter of dishes, the clink of tinny silverware, and she was hungry. Ha, she had an idea. Slowly she raised her legs back to the bed, turned, and crawled on all fours to the foot of the bed until she was even with the wheelchair, then turned again and sat down with her legs dangling over the side. She examined the wheelchair with calculating eyes. If she placed her feet on the footrest, it would topple over on its large wheels. How could she get her behind over the armrest and onto the seat? Impossible. She felt helpless, frustrated. Where was Ben, the darnfool? She needed him. Ruth stared out the doorway, saw a nurse hurrying past, opened her mouth to call out, but the nurse disappeared in a rush. Why don't you call out, you timid little wretch? She listened to the clatter of dishes, heard voices raised. She was helpless. Ring the bell, someone will come. To the devil with them! Glanced again at the wheelchair a mere few inches away. Had they forgotten her? Damn them! Tomorrow she'd have to start learning how to walk again. She placed her hands and weight on the armrest but the chair rolled slightly. It was too precarious. Call out! Ring the bell! Where was Ben? Harry? She felt the blood rush to her head, her heart beat wildly. Ruth was in a panic now, one hand on the wheelchair, her feet dangling, a pain in her hip, all alone, helpless, frustrated, frightened, beads of perspiration rolling down her cheeks. Don't be bashful, you fool, call out!

Ruth just couldn't do it—a lifetime interfered.

Tears burned in her eyes, her heart beat harshly against her ribs, her face was on fire, and now her hip hurt with the pain of a jagged knife sawing at her bones. Her head was dizzy, ready to burst. She closed her eyes. Tried to control her panic. Felt two strong hands on her shoulders. Opened her eyes. It was Ben Stein, smiling gently at her. Ruth immediately felt cool; the panic slipped quickly away.

"Time for supper," she said, smiling at him.

"What's your hurry, not yet, it's only three o'clock, time for a glass of tea," he whispered in his grating voice, and grabbing her under the armpits helped her into the wheelchair, not forgetting as he withdrew his hands to brush them against her old breasts. She smiled to herself.

After supper Ruth couldn't sleep. She lay propped up in her bed hawking bitter phlegm and spitting it out into the little crescent-shaped enameled basin. There was a horrid taste at the bottom of her throat, a heartburn in her chest, and a terrible pain in her belly. It hurt, really hurt.

Ben Stein sat near the bed, observing her mournfully.

"What was it the doctor said?" she asked, though she had heard the doctor very clearly.

Because her face was turned from him, Ben couldn't read her lips, so he said nothing. She faced him and repeated her question.

"He said you should not eat so much," the old man replied in his harsh whisper.

Ruth closed her eyes, sneering disgustedly to herself. Ben was too kind to repeat exactly what the doctor had said. "You eat like a pig. I told you a hundred times you have high blood pressure, you have an hiatus hernia, your body can't take all that food. From now on we will put you on a strict diet. You won't even get an extra slice of bread." Then the doctor had smiled kindly. "Don't worry, Mrs. Elias, we're no longer living in the depression, there'll be enough food for the next meal." Shaking his head, he patted her hand, spoke to the nurse, and left.

The nurse spoonfed her a large dose of white chalk, fetched an extra pillow and propped her up. "It will go down soon, Ruth, and you'll feel better," and left busily with a swish of white. As the nurse departed, Monkeyface entered. Really, she wished he would go away now. Who wanted to look at his mournful face? To speak to him was an effort she did not want to make, and if she was going to remain silent, who needed him? She was her own best company, and if he wasn't here she could complain and moan all she wanted.

Ruth gazed woefully at Ben and he smiled. He certainly was a monkeyface with his tiny eyes and pouched upper lip and flat nose. Ruth was on the verge of asking him please to go away but couldn't get up the energy to be mean. All her life she couldn't get up the energy to be mean. For that very reason everyone thought she was a fool. She knew, she had seen it in their faces. Mean people were rarely thought to be fools. Kind people, decent people, unselfish people, they could be thought to be fools. Mean people were mean, not fools. You could hate mean people, but that was all. What a fool, you might say of a person who had done a kind deed for a mean one. But if a mean person did a kind deed, oh, my God, you see, underneath he is a decent human being. She, Ruth Elias, would have been much better off if all her life she had been mean. They would have respected her more. Her husband, her sisters, her neighbors, even her children. Her firstborn, Jack, would be on the phone every week and writing letters twice a month. Look at Fanny Golan with her fat outspread thighs and rouged face—at her age. A real mean one. But *her* Jack writes, phones, comes to visit—oh, boy, *his* mother. If a plague descended from heaven and pocked Fanny Golan from head to toe, she, Ruth Elias, would laugh, Ha, good for her.

"Ben," Ruth said, turning to him, "why don't you go and listen to TV, Bob Hope is a guest star on NBC. He will make you laugh."

Ben smiled sadly, whispered, "Bob Hope? He talks too fast, I can't read his lips. So how can I laugh?"

"All right, sit here then. I will make you laugh."

"Are you feeling better?"

"No. Yes. A little bit. It's going down." Why didn't he take the hint? He was nice, he was a fool.

Ruth dozed, woke up, stared into nothing. Her life was passing, second by second, doing nothing, a lump, like some strange creature at the bottom of the sea, sunk deep into the sand, never moving, sucking particles of food as they drifted past, sucking air from the water, defecating, the weight of her life endlessly rolling and rocking over her. Gone were the precious moments of life, gaiety, tragedy, the stirrings of creation in her belly, an infant at her breast, children laughing and crying, fighting, that was life, too. Mom, when do we eat? Mom, what's there to eat? Mom, why does she have to borrow my blouse, that's the only decent one I have, goddamn her? Ma, can I have a penny for a tootsie roll? For Christ's sake, Ma, can't *he* wash the dishes for once? The coal stove orange hot, snow on the window sills, on the trees, the roofs. The children in their underwear, their longies. Her birthday. To Ma. For Mom. To My Mother with Love. From your loving son, Jack. From your Becky who loves you. Becky, Becky, I love you, too, honest I do. You must forget the terrible words I spoke to you. Better I had lost my tongue before I uttered them. The skinny, bony little girl with the long thin legs, thick long hair, her eyes huge and sunk deep into the bony skull, her dress a patched rag, snot dripping from her Volodin nose. A Roman nose, they called it, ha! Becky crying without tears. "Mama, how could you say that?" Turning away from the child, angry, in a fury, none of the other children saying a word, Becky standing there forlornly, sniffling, the snot dripping, the eyes huge and cavernous, then running from the kitchen to hide under the wooden backstairs of the three-decker, not returning for hours.

She should have spoken to the child then, immediately,

told her she was sorry, she didn't mean it, but she had never spoken, never said a word to the child about it ever again, and now it was too late.

What terrible thing had the child done? "Mama loves Shep. Shep loves Mama." In white chalk, in a heart, on the sidewalk in front of the house. All the neighbors knew anyway, so what did it matter?

"You horrible child, who wanted you, who needed you, I had enough children! Too many children!"

The truth. But is the truth always the truth? And must the truth always be said? It is better that some truths die in one's heart. And especially to a child. And more especially to Becky because Becky had been the least wanted of her children. That was the one she didn't want. She had wept and stormed when she became pregnant with her until even Reuben had become frightened and brought her pills that Sam Sunshine, the druggist and comrade, gave him. She had taken them all at one time and all that had happened was that she ran and ran to the toilet, emptied out her insides, but not Becky. Becky held on like a bloodsucking leech. The truth was that while Becky was in her womb, she hated her. But the truth also was that after Becky was born she loved her as much as she loved her other children. Becky was born, she kicked and she howled, she sucked at her breasts, she smiled, she laughed, she clung. Why shouldn't she, Ruth, love her? Becky was her child.

It had been Reuben's fault. Things had become so bad that he couldn't endure it any longer. He could have closed his mouth and kept a job for once in his life. The revolution. His revolution. Where was it? And where it was what good did it do? They built some factories and killed millions. A big blessing. Paradise. A Jew can't even bake a piece of matzoh. But that was what he believed, dear man, and couldn't keep his mouth shut. So things were even worse for them than for others, and Reuben couldn't endure it any longer. He took to drinking like a peasant, where he obtained the money, God knows. Homemade whiskey. A new plague. A drunken husband. She couldn't stand his breath, the stink, the trembling hands, the slurred speech, the violence. All her childhood she had lived in fear of being raped by a drunken peasant. Now she lived with one. For once she screamed. For once she rebelled. For once she beat him with her fists and spit in his face. But he was as strong as an ox and had his way with her body, once, twice, three times, who knows? Then abruptly he caught hold of himself. Stopped drinking. He was a strong-willed man, he was not really a drunkard. But too late, she was pregnant. And too late for something else. Why did she think about it now? It had lain tucked away, hidden, forgotten, until it never even existed. Now it returned as wretched as the pain in her chest.

It was afternoon. A half-drunk Reuben and she had fought, screamed, and he had run heavily from the house. She could still hear his faltering steps going down the backstairs and remember her wish that he fall and break his mulish neck. She sat at the kitchen table weeping. Then she heard a light step in the room behind her and then tender hands caressing her hair. It was Shep, of course. He held her weeping head to his thin chest, tenderly caressing her hair, her cheeks. It was the first time he had ever touched her. He was merely a boy, perhaps twenty-one or two and she was in her thirties. Then as in a dream he led her to her bedroom, her and Reuben's bed, and she let him, as if still in a dream, and then as she pretended to sleep he left before anyone returned. She had committed adultery, she had sinned against her husband, her children, her God. When Reuben returned she was still weeping and he begged forgiveness, vowed he wouldn't drink anymore, but for the first few days afterwards she couldn't look at him, avoided his eyes, wept endless hours, found it impossible to sleep.

When Shep visited several days later she of course told him he was never again to come when no one was home—and he never did, not until months after Reuben's death many years later. Reuben did not immediately keep his vow, and that month she found herself pregnant and she thought she would go out of her mind. She hated the foetus in her womb, she trembled for the foetus in her womb. The seed of adultery or of a drunken man? God knew what the child would be. A mongolian idiot. Sickly. With a balloon head filled with water like the poor Kleins down the street had been cursed with. Who could tell?

The doctor in the clinic tried to reassure her (she had not told him about Shep, only about Reuben's drinking), but did doctors tell the truth? She tried to rid herself of the child. Worked like a horse scrubbing floors, walls, clothes. The baby grew huge in her stomach. It was a horrible time for her, for Reuben, for many of his comrades. The government was hunting down Bolsheviks, anarchists, bomb-throwers. Rumor had it that Reuben had been involved with Sacco and Vanzetti. But they were anarchists, and Reuben had become a Bolshevik and hated the anarchists. Reuben sobered up quickly. "We move to the farm," he said.

So they went to live with her sister Lilly on the farm she and her husband Sam Boxer owned outside Chicopee. They had a vegetable garden, a cow, some chickens, so there was something to eat. The house was heated with wood and coal stoves; kerosene was used for light; there was an outhouse for two and a water pump outside the kitchen door.

In return for the two rooms in which the Elias family lived and for the use of the barn, Reuben worked hard to put the house, the sheds, and the barn into good repair. She, Jack, about nine at the time, and Sophie, six, helped in the vegetable garden and with the chickens. Polly, sweet child, was just a toddler. Lilly, who was not very strong, did her share. Still, Boxer, whose fledgling insurance office adjoined the kitchen, kept the door open a crack and groaned everytime the icebox was opened.

If Boxer was a miser, Reuben was a tsar. Not only did she have to take care of the three children, carry pails of water in from the pump, work in the vegetable garden, wash clothes, cook, keep the house clean (Lilly, poor woman, helped as best she could), but she had to make sure Reuben's white shirt and stiff collar were always starched and ironed, his one pair of good trousers pressed, his fedora brushed, his one pair of good shoes polished, his socks darned. After supper every evening, Reuben would bathe himself with cold water from the pump and dress in his starched white shirt. With his black curly hair brilliant from the wetness, his felt hat at a rakish turn, the horse hitched to the wagon, off he'd go to secret Party meetings, to talkfests with his friends, to great quantities of hot tea and black raspberry jam, to smiles at the ladies.

What else did he do that kept him away till all hours of the early morning? She never knew. And if she knew, then what? Could she have divorced him? Because he gave another lady a—a—Ruth couldn't say the word. Divorce was for the rich and the sinful. Mrs. Lupowitz gave her her divorce. Aaa . . .

Food was scarce. The cow became ill and dried up. Whatever milk there was, Lilly, poor soul, tried to save for the Elias children and for her, Ruth, who was now as round as she was tall. Soon there would be another. Not a blond child, she hoped, please, God, not a blond, but hair as black as pitch. . . . Boxer liked milk, too. One day there was only half a quart left in the pail in the icebox. Lilly guarded it with her life—but the outhouse called. As she sat on the cold wood seat, she heard a floorboard squeak. With quick anger, her job only half done, she rushed into the kitchen to catch Boxer swallowing the last drop. Lilly was a timid woman, even more timid than she, but this flagrant unkindness was too much for her and she screeched and wept at this mean beast of a man she had married, so that even he lowered his bitter, cold eyes and left.

Perhaps his guilt further embittered him, for late that afternoon when Reuben returned from Southbridge where he'd gone with a friend who had a car to find work at the optical plant—hoping they hadn't heard of him, they had and turned him down—Boxer couldn't conceal his contempt and berated Reuben mercilessly.

"You lazy bum, you Bolshevik, you're blacklisted in every factory in Massachusetts. You'll never get a job, you're worthless, you ought to go back to Russia where you belong." On and on he ranted.

Reuben listened until every last contemptuous word was out. For months he'd been restraining his temper. Now at last he broke loose. His short brawny arms waving wildly, his black hair falling over his eyes, he screamed, "You piece of shit, you green turd, you filth, you scum, you plague, you haven't a human nerve in your piggish body. You have a stone heart and a wooden cock . . ."

In the kitchen the children hid behind her skirts as she and Lilly rocked from side to side like mourners before the Wall. Boxer stood tall before Reuben, not a muscle twitching, a stone monument, his eyes colder and colder. Suddenly he turned and strode into the barn. With his stiff constipated movements he hitched the horse, climbed to the high seat and with a cruel slash whipped the animal. Out the barn door the horse flew, never giving Boxer a chance to duck. Even the house shook from the force of the whack.

Reuben had already entered the house and begun changing clothes. Lilly ran from the kitchen to see what had happened, and all she could see was the driverless horse and wagon disappearing down the dirt road that ran between the high grass and weeds. With superhuman swiftness she ran down the road, her long skirts flying behind her. In and about the high grass she searched, screaming, "Boxer, Boxer, where are you? Oh, Boxer, my husband, where are you?"

Finally, between a clump of skunkweed and tall sunflower stalks, she found her husband. From her throat issued a long, thin, reedy wail. "Oh, God in heaven, he is dead!"

They ran, she, Reuben, Jack, Sophie and even the tiny Polly, as quickly as they could to Lilly's side. They found her lying in a heap next to Boxer. His forehead was split open and his back broken, but he was not dead.

Sam Boxer was taken to the hospital in Springfield. For days he lay unconscious, his heart very much alive, the remainder of him paralyzed. When she went to visit him and saw this powerful, handsome man so utterly broken, she cried. But Boxer refused to allow anyone to believe that pain could defeat him. "Don't cry, Ruth," he whispered, "I'm all right, I'll be well again." That was Boxer, the miser, he couldn't even allow her the solace of crying for him, but she had to admit he was a brave man. He held on to life as strongly as he held on to a dollar.

Boxer lived. Regained use of his arms, his neck, his back. Only his legs remained useless. He refused help from anyone. Using his muscular shoulders and arms, his courage and pride, he would manage to climb into his wheelchair and go about his business. He refused to have a telephone installed, it was too expensive, so Lilly became his legs, his messenger girl, and within a few years, despite the depression, Boxer became one of the wealthiest men in western Massachusetts. More hateful, more mean, only Lilly, may she rest in peace, remained loyal to him.

Sometimes, to give Lilly a plum, he would take her to the movies, but he must always get her there before five o'clock, when the price changed from ten to fifteen cents. Late one afternoon, shortly after a heavy snowfall, she begged him to take her to see Charlie Chaplin. Finally, he consented, ordering her to shovel the snow which blocked the barn doors. She set to with a rush. "Hurry," he called, "or we'll have to pay more." Lilly shoveled as quickly as she could. The chore completed, she turned to pull open the barn door and fell dead of a heart attack, dear sister, her pinched face once beautiful like that of a porcelain doll.

. . . A no-good bastard, just a no-good bastard!

While Boxer was still in the hospital after the accident, the family came from New York, from Utica, from Buffalo to console Lilly in her misfortune. They chose the weekend of the Fourth for their visit, and came all at one time on the train to Springfield. Reuben brought them in the large hay wagon to the Boxer farm. She, her belly ready to burst, Jack, and Sophie had to run around to find enough pillows and linen to make beds on the floor, on two chairs, on the sofa, on old mattresses dragged from the barn loft, while Lilly was at the hospital sitting meekly at Boxer's side as he glared stone-faced and mean.

They all arrived; they were tired, hungry, and she worked, the serf with the pregnant belly. They kissed her, oh, they were so tired, washed at the pump, changed their clothes. Jack and Sophie, young and little as they were, helped her. Polly sat on the floor playing with the rag doll Jack had made for her. They ate. Reuben entertained the guests with songs, anecdotes, and talk of the revolution, swinging from one to the other with great facility. Also taunting them. "Jews. Always crying. I'm not a Jew, I'm an atheist." Foolish man, admit it, truly a foolish man. He was born a Jew and died a Jew in every fiber of his stalwart body. But his guests, who knew him well, merely lowered their eyes, drank scorching hot tea from glasses in the ninety degree heat of summer, and patiently waited until he turned his quick mind to another subject. Another song, perhaps. He had a voice like Caruso's.

As she baked bread in the oven, walked heavily about the kitchen, she could feel the baby stir inside her. Soon she would know whose child it was. It was due. Today, tomorrow. She could feel it. But she didn't say a word. She was possessed of an idiot pride that prevented her from crying out in anger, rebelling, showing her discomfort, because it would be like stooping, pleading for attention. Why don't they see my pain? I see theirs. Why don't they give me some notice, I give it to them. Sometimes you have to ask for what is due you because most people are too busy thinking of what's coming to them. If you don't ask, they think you don't care. And then you hold it inside like a bitter secret, full of gall, and when you finally let it out it's always against yourself, ripping the skin off your nails, picking at yourself until you bleed.

She labored like a mule all day of the third of July; no one paid her attention as she pumped water, carried full pails in each hand, cooked, cleaned, picked vegetables with Jack, a ragged skinny little boy with huge black eyes, with Sophie minding the little Polly. Reuben forgot to milk the new cow, and she even had to do that for fear of raising his anger.

The following morning, Lilly and little Sophie helped her make breakfast for everyone. Jack carefully found the eggs laid by the hens, and then they all left for the hospital, taking Sophie with them. They hoped to cheer up Boxer, perhaps even get him to sing duets with Reuben to forget his pain. When Boxer sang it was with the voice of Chaliapin, and his eyes came alive. He was human, after all. When Boxer and Reuben sang together the world stood still to listen. They left the skinny Jack, the quiet one with the smoldering eyes, and the tiny Polly to look after their mother. And she knew the baby was about to be born and didn't say a word. She hated all of them for not seeing what was obvious but said nothing. Only she knew. She made the beds, cleaned the kitchen, and the small life inside her howled to see light.

To the devil with them all, she would take care of herself. Two hands grasping the empty pails, Jack playing with Polly in the sand, she shouldered open the kitchen door, carried her heavy body to the water pump. The sun was high, not a weed moved, the air was still, not a sound but Polly's piping giggle as Jack made her rag doll stand on its head, the sky's blue blinding. In the distance, round the bend of the dirt road, the neighboring farmer's new tractor, the very first in the area, clanked and roared. Mr. Wojinski was so proud, even though his wife was crazy, was a dope fiend, or so Reuben said. She pumped one pail full, then the second. She bent her knees to lift them, stood straight, and her water burst and her thighs were wet, and she could feel the baby slip down. She dropped the pails. The pain came swiftly, sharp, like a knife across her abdomen, a knife deep under her lower spine. She screamed. Her time had come. The baby raged to see light. Another knife, sharply jagged, raked across her womb. She lay on the grass to have her child like a peasant in the field.

"Jack," she called. "Come quickly, child!" Jack stood over her, his bony face scared.

"Quick, run to the crazy lady . . . call the doctor. Hurry. For Mama, Jack."

The little boy stared at her, his eyes wide, frightened. Another knife, sharper, from her very center up the length of her body to her throat. The baby was now pressing like a thousand pound weight. "Run, child, sweet boy, run quickly. Please."

Finally, her little son came to life, turned and fled down the road. Polly stood over her, staring sadly, offered her rag doll to her mother. She tried to smile at the child, then screamed again. The child stood petrified, staring at her mother screaming on the ground.

Jack ran fast, dear boy. Round the bend to the red farmhouse where Wojinski's crazy lady lived. Dope fiend, Reuben called her. Jack punched his stick legs faster, his fists clutched to his heart. There was the red house and barns, he was up to them, and he saw the crazy lady, her blond hair like a hen's nest, sitting with her back against the big tree, staring dazedly into space. "Lady, please . . . Mama . . . quick . . . call the doctor. Please!" The crazy lady, the dope fiend, screwed her eyes shut, opened them, shook her head, the odor, Jack was to say years later, from her mouth like old garbage.

"Hello, Jack darling, come sit with me."

"Mama's baby is coming . . . quick . . . call the doctor."

The crazy lady squeezed her eyes shut, again shook her head, opened her eyes.

"Please, my mama's screaming. It hurts."

At last she heard the words. "Oh, Mother of God." Mrs. Wojinski leaped to her feet and ran like a shot into her house to call the doctor. The doctor was at a Fourth of July celebration getting drunk, but at last was reached.

Jack sat with tiny Polly near her as she lay in the grass, her legs spread apart, her skirts raised high and the baby half out, covered with streaks of blood and shiny white matter. The children sat there silent, wide-eyed, Polly hugging her rag doll to her chest, as her mother was screaming and screaming. Suddenly she stopped and sighed and the baby quietly slid out. Shortly after cleaned by a half-drunken doctor who by pure instinct didn't harm a hair on her head.

Hair neither black nor blond, but fiery red like her own, but the eyes black as pitch, Reuben's child, thank God. Healthy, knock on wood, perfectly formed, beautiful like all her children.

She tucked the incident with Shep deep inside her. Forgot about it, it never happened. Then, like an explosion, it burst out in a rage years later when she screamed at Becky, "Who wanted you?" A wound in a child's life.

Jack once told her that one's brain never forgets anything, it all rests there, concealed. Someone presses the button, the wrong one, the right one, and there it is. There it rested in Becky's brain, concealed, and she, Ruth, could only pray the wrong button would never be pressed. Why should one of Becky's children, or whoever, some day feel the hurt that Becky's mother had once inflicted on her? My God, it could go on from child to child into eternity. One major sin. One moment of rage. One injury. When God made the first woman and the first man did He know what He was doing? A plumber, a shoemaker without thumbs.

Maybe tomorrow I will phone Becky, Ruth thought, knowing she never would, and ask her to forgive me, then perhaps she will think twice before passing it on. Then she, Ruth, could sleep better, be at peace with herself whenever she thought of Becky. It was too late to apologize to Shep for not caring enough to see that he went to the doctor for coughing up blood. She would go to her grave with that sorrow heavy on her heart.

Ruth groaned, hawked up phlegm, a little less bitter now. Her chest still felt constricted, but the heartburn was mostly gone.

She moved her head the better to observe Ben Stein. He sat on the chair like a lump on a log, bump on a log, who cares? Deaf he was, but he could speak, so why didn't he? What was he thinking about? The same thing she was thinking about—the past. His meannesses, his sins, his inflicted injuries, his children, his life. Old people thought of the past. Young people thought of the moment. Middle-aged people thought of the past, the moment, and still had enough left over to think of the future—if not their own, at least their children's. Which part of life was the most sorrowful? Every part of it. Which part was the most happy?

Certainly not the last part. Perhaps the first part, but not for all of them. The middle part, but also not for all of them. Happiness is a fairy tale, so thank God for fairy tales!

In the middle of nothing, Ben Stein smiled at her, his little monkeyface a concentric circle of deep wrinkles. His tiny eyes beamed at her, and his eyebrows rose high as if he had just remembered something. "I will be right back, Ruth."

He rose, sprightly for an old man, straight as a soldier, and ran from the room. Before she had time to wonder, she could hear him returning—his door was only two down—and then he reentered carrying a little gift-wrapped package, purple, with a yellow ribbon.

He stood at her side, his eyes intent upon her as he handed it to her. "This is for you, Ruth. A present."

Ruth pretended surprise. "For me?" And unwrapped it slowly as it lay on her lap. It was the purse he had been making, all finished. "How beautiful, Ben. Lovely. You made it?"

"I made it myself. For you, Ruth." He was smiling happily, as she opened it and examined the inside.

"Good workmanship, Ben, you have a good pair of hands." She was smiling at him and she could see he was very proud of his handiwork.

"Oh, I forgot," he whispered, plunged his knobby hand into his pocket, and extracted a half dollar. He took the purse from her, snapped it open, and dropped the coin in. "For good luck, Ruth," he said, laying it in her lap.

Ruth smiled fondly at him. "Thank you very much, it's just what I needed. Becky was supposed to buy me one," she lied, "but forgot, for when I go home." Ruth played the old game. Ben and she both knew they were never going home, but it was pleasant to pretend they were.

Silent now, not knowing what else to say, they faced one another. But Ruth had to admit to herself that for a moment there had been happiness—not much, a little. Sometimes a little was a whole lot. Perhaps they could enlarge it, make it endure a moment longer. Old as they were, they were human, not beasts.

Ruth raised her old hands, the ravaged skin and flesh falling away from the bones, and took Ben's head and pressed his wrinkled monkeyface to her aged one. She could feel his tears on her skin and her own in her eyes. Of happiness? Of sorrow? Who cared, so long as it was something they felt.

The old-age home was quiet except for the rasping snores of the aged. The night staff of nurses and attendants sat in the dimly lighted solarium talking quietly among themselves, drinking coffee or tea. The pre-dawn sky lay a dull purple over the rooftops.

In his small room, Louis Friedman slept in a half-empty double bed and dreamt of his Molke who would never return. In her room, ancient Sarah wore a silk nightgown, and around her chin was tied a silk ribbon; her snore was delicate as befitted a great beauty. Miss Marian Ross, the old schoolteacher, had slept her usual four hours, and now wrapped in a blue flannel bathrobe sat on a straight chair under an excellent light reading from her leatherbound copy of *Silas Marner*. Sally Berman slept on a rubber pad fortunately still dry after so many hours, and her friend Fanny Golan lay on her back snoring noisily as she dreamt of her loving son Jack. Izzy Smith passed a poor night, waking every half hour or so to seek out the time, for he was terrified of dying in his sleep.

In the solarium the staff heard a door squeak down at the other end of the polished corridor. An attendant craned his neck, squinted, saw Ben Stein, the wiry little rooster, slip from his room and pad towards Ruth Elias's door. The attendant smiled to himself, returned to the conversation.

Ben entered Ruth's room, closed the door softly behind him and in the gray-purple darkness found his way to her bed.

Ruth awoke with a moan, was it already time to get washed? She recognized Ben and smiled sleepily.

"I couldn't sleep anymore," he said in his harsh whisper.

Ruth moved heavily towards the wall, made room in her bed for him. "So what are you waiting for?" she said.

Slowly he climbed in.

They lay side by side for a few minutes, then he turned towards her and Ruth accepted his small aged body into her old arms, then sighing deeply received his gentle kindness as well.

NINA—3

Dear Mom & Dad,

Hello again. Things are going very well for the most
part. My classes are pretty good, except for English which
is fantastic. I'm finding geometry easy and French III
really hard. But I guess I'm bound to have trouble with
something. The girls who've been my friends so far have
grown closer. My favorite is a girl named Rita Wrong
(you can see what she has to live with)—a curlyheaded
comedienne who's on the first floor, but I see her less
often as she's not in any of my classes. Abbey Pyle, who's
one of the most beautiful girls I've ever seen, is a good
friend, but she's become close to Tom Lawrence so I only
see her during the day.

I'm trying not to let the boys bug me, but it's hard.
There really isn't any pressure to have a boy friend but
when boys are around constantly, and one's friends are
always found studying, walking, and talking with boys, it
is sort of difficult to ignore them and run back to a girl
friend. Rita Wrong and I stick together when we're both
free, so I've got her to fall back on, and I really have fun
with her. It sounds like I'm a wallflower. (I know, Dad,
don't get excited, I've only been here a short time.) Actually, a lot of boys say hello, but all of them are either assholes or they've got another girl they're really interested
in, and so they don't pay any attention to me unless I
happen to see them in the hall or something. There is one
kid who seems to adore me, but, unfortunately, I can't
stand him. It is so embarrassing to have this creep hang-

ing all over you when you're trying to talk to someone worthwhile. And he doesn't seem to get the point although I'm constantly breaking off our little conversations with a "Well, gotta go. Bye," and I flash down the stairs. Oh, well, things can't get any worse in the male department, so perhaps they'll start getting better.

Another thing that's been troubling me is that I'm quickly losing all confidence in myself. I am virtually surrounded by either blond Miss Americas like Abbey Pyle or brunette calendar girls like Carol. (She's the one who's always bragging about how many guys she's made out with.) I've seen only two girls who look even faintly Jewish. Oh, there's one Jewish girl in our dorm, but she's a ninth grader only and a very immature one at that— nice, but really not a person I'd like to be friendly with. Anyhow, back to the beauties. I'm honestly beginning to doubt I'm at all nice looking, but of course it's ridiculous, I'm just weird looking in relation to everyone else around here. But the boys won't even bother getting to know any girl who doesn't have the good looks to attract them to begin with. I guess eventually I'll get to know boys and at that point we'll be friends, instead of the other way around. But I suppose my not being top dog or near top dog is a good thing for me, only I really don't find it very pleasant. I'll keep you posted anyhow as to how my ego is getting along.

While I'm forgetting to accentuate the positive like that old song Pops loves to hear so much on the record player, I might as well go all the way into the negative. I'm beginning to feel like li'l ole Cinderella around here. My friend Louise is half Ford Motors and half Frick Museum! Rita Wrong lives on Park Avenue and her mother came to visit in a chauffeur-driven white ROLLS ROYCE!!! And there are a couple more like that. In fact, Marcy, my black friend, and me are the poorest ones in our class. Those rich kids are pretty decent, though, and don't walk around with their tiny noses up in the air, but how can I help but notice that their closets are filled with loads of brand-new clothes and that when we go to town I have to count my pennies before I buy something and they never even stop to think before they lay out a ten-dollar bill. And and and. I know, Dad, I asked for it, so I got it. Just don't rub it in, because I'm getting a fantastic education which is what I came here for after hearing all those complaints Eli and Pete made about how boring Highview High was.

Today Rita, Abbey, Carol, and another kid named Nina, and I went to Friendly's for sundaes. I bought myself two honeydew melons on the way back, so now I'll just have melon for breakfast, and Abbey has granola so sometimes I'll splurge and have that, too. Dinners have gotten better, no fried turds lately, chicken one night, a not bad at all filet of sole last night, and once in a while we get apples or pears for dessert. It isn't Rebecca Miller's famous cuisine, but it will have to do.

How's the day care center work going, Mom? They are the cutest little things. Are you getting used to me being away? Dad, I got your letter. Don't worry about me becoming snobby. I'll never forget I come from a working-class family and that I'm a Jew. You never let me forget the first and my weird looks the second. (One kid from Texas never saw a Jew before, can you believe it, he thought I was an American Indian.) I miss you both so much, and I guess I also miss the freedom one has at home. But I'm happy here. Give my best love to my little cat Davey.

Love and kisses,
Nina xxxxxxxx

P.S. I need: raincoat, flag, pink flannel long nightgown, bandaids, fruit, store bought granola. You can bring this stuff when you come up for a visit—soon, I hope, Mummy. Oh—and a few of my James Taylor records. Write soon, empty P.O. boxes are very depressing. I receive letters from Eli, but none from Pete, of course, since the first one. Has Diogenes gone off again? I sent another letter to Nanny Ruth. I hate that place, just hate it, it's gross. Bring homemade cookies, also, will you, Momsie? More kisses. Mom, I forgot to tell you the last time I saw you you should stop biting your lips and drumming with your fingers so much when you're nervous. They give you away. And Daddy, don't give in to those prejudiced Southern white guys when you go to North Carolina. I know you won't but I thought I should tell you anyway.

xxxxxxxNeen

LIFE—HOW MUCH DOES IT COST?

When Peter Reuben Miller was a little boy there was a game he played with his mother as foil.

"Tough," he'd say.
"What's tough?"
"Life."
"What's life?"
"A magazine."
"Where do you get it?"
"At a newsstand."
"How much does it cost?"
"A quarter."
"Only got a dime."
"Tough."
"What's tough?"
"Life."
Et cetera, et cetera.

Now he was a man, or at least so he thought.

He woke up, stared at the asbestos-covered steam pipes running overhead, coughed up some phlegm, rolled it around his mouth. He dropped a hand over the side of the bed, groped for and found the box of tissues on the floor. Empty. As usual. Try to remember to buy a new box. Swallowed the phlegm. Back where it came from. Life is circular. From dust to dust. He hawked up some more phlegm—or perhaps the very same gob—this time spat it on the littered floor. Ought to stop smoking. Yeah, next year. He had enough things saved up for next year to take him at least twenty years to accomplish.

He sat up. Plunged his big Miller mitts through his red hair, found his oily scalp after a frantic search, explored it, and scratched. Maybe I can find a sickle mower on Barrow Street and give myself a haircut. With the drought and all perhaps I can get a dollar a bale, have enough money for a couple of days. He sighed. Could always hit Pop for a few. And hear a lecture. If Pop hit the lecture circuit he'd make a million.

Pete swung his gluey eyes to the narrow basement window. All he saw was grime and darkness. He bet the window hadn't seen sun since the day the building was built eighty years ago. He dropped his hand again over the side of the bed and found his dollar watch on the floor and peered at it squint-eyed in the semi-darkness. Its hands were motionless. I'll fix that.

After a futile ten minute search through the dresser drawers he found his penknife in his trouser pocket, sat on the dust-covered floor with legs crossed, the watch in one hand and the knife in the other. Slowly, patiently, he disassembled the watch, placing its various parts on the floor haphazardly. He saw that the spring was loose, had lost its curl. Holding it delicately in his thick fingers, tongue between teeth, he twisted the spring so it became taut. There, that's it. Like new. The last dying fly of August made an imperfect landing on his sweaty forehead and he moved to brush it off with the back of his hand. The watch spring sprung sprightly from between his fingers and landed in a puff of dust between two floor boards. He ran the knife blade along the crack until he found the spring and pried it up. It leaped and bounced under the bed, he after it like an agile cat, but not as cautiously, for he scraped his naked back on the iron bedstead which he'd bought at Jake's Junk for three dollars. "Son of a bitch," he yelled, but the spring refused to reveal itself. "Vile little bastard," he muttered, backing out angrily from under the bed, this time banging the base of his skull. No pain. Saved by the hay. Very functional. The long hair battle had been won years ago, so there was little reason to let it grow. Still I will not cut it. I shall not cut it. He wrinkled his brow, stood, and padded across the room to a pile of books on the floor near a wall, closed his eyes and unerringly came up with *Fowler's Modern Usage*. Bought a few years before when, like all his friends, he thought he was going to be a writer. Started to open it, gave it up as too hazardous. I won't cut my hair. Suddenly remembered Fowler. "I will be drowned, no one shall save me." I shall go to work, no one will stop me.

Peter sat on the bed, lifted a black sock, slid his foot into it. Four toes protruded but he barely noticed. The second sock—and the heel was nonexistent. Stepped into his trousers, buckled them on, forgot to zip the zipper. Stuck his head into a green polo shirt but it caught in what turned out to be a hole under the sleeve. Poked around and finally found the alleged collar. At the door he stepped into a pair of crushed Hush Puppies that looked like they'd been boiled and then hung up to dry. For no reason he could think of he kicked first one and then the other off and followed their parabolic flight. They landed one alongside the other under the window. He laughed and raised the first and then the second of his feet to remove his so-called socks. Started to open the door to the furnace room, and so outward bound, and abruptly for no apparent reason thought of his mother—the patient, saintly Rebecca Miller—so good, so understanding that just standing before her looking into her face you felt guilty enough to want to jump off the roof for not having brushed your teeth. Goddamn her, why didn't she yell just once so you could yell back and feel better? The smiling lady. The Great Pacifier! Clammed up. Like mother, like son. At least the old man yelled his bloody head off and then crushed you in his arms—tried to browbeat and then batter his way into you. Didn't they understand he was scared shitless? Of what? Who knows?

Peter felt the tears burning at the rims of his eyes, so he closed the door, retraced his steps to the bed and sat down and said aloud, "What a fucking hell we live in." He lay back and stared at the steam pipes running under the low ceiling. If they burst the hell wouldn't be any steamier than the hell in his brain. He remembered the last real conversation he'd had with his father. Some friend of his mother's—the ass-swiveling Liz Morrison—had been to the house and before leaving had said, "Peter, you look like Michelangelo's David." He'd nodded stupidly at her—what else can you do when some so-called adult says that to you?

After she left, his father kidded him about it, and, smiling, he responded, "Except I like girls. Though I make no judgment about boys who don't."

Suddenly for no obvious reason—parents always think they are very subtle—his father said, "Have you thought about what you're going to do?"

"I'm too lazy."

"Have you thought about it?"

"Yeah—that's why I said I was too lazy. I think about it and don't do anything about it. . . . Right now, I prefer working with my hands."

"Come on, now, all you kids—"

"I won't go back to college, Dad."

"I didn't—"

"You were about to."

With a laugh, the lid over his glass eye drooping, his father said, "You're right."

"I'm sorry, but I don't have to go just because you didn't."

"You'll become bored pounding nails, ask any man who has to do it for a living."

"I haven't asked you for any money, have I?"

"No. But you know—"

"Yeah, you're right again, I'm always aware I can get a few bucks from you or Mom."

"Just so much, kiddo. The union pays me a decent salary, but I don't take graft. I'm an honest porkchopper, besides I—"

"Some day I'll sit down and think seriously about my life."

"Don't do it to please me."

"I never do anything to please you."

"Don't rub it in." Then looking at him from the corner of his good eye, his old man said, "You lie on occasion, don't you?"

"Yeah, but that's so you and Mom won't worry or be hurt."

"Stop patronizing us."

"Parents have to be protected from their wayward children."

"Go to hell, you little bastard."

"I'm taller than you are. Sometimes, Dad—"

"Go ahead, say it, don't protect me."

"Sometimes I think I'm already there."

"I'm not following you."

"In hell, Dad, in hell!"

And that damned aging bull had looked at him with a terrible sadness, muttered something under his breath that sounded like, "Damnfool kid," and abruptly grabbed him in his strong arms and kissed his forehead. "I've been there and back many times myself and so will you and there's not a thing anyone else can do about it."

He, Peter, had cried a bit, sniffled, wiped his nose, his father just holding him to his chest.

Now Peter rested in the warmth of that memory for a few minutes, then, reinvigorated, ventured forth.

The door closed behind him, and the acrid odor of garbage blinded him momentarily. He wiped his eyes, then held his nose between two dirty fingers. Out on the street, the sidewalk was hot to his bare feet, but he liked the feel of it, was accustomed to it. The sun forced him to slit his eyes so its garish light would filter through the foliage of his thick eyelashes. The girls always mentioned his eyelashes. They were long, curly, and tarnished gold.

He was greeted at the door of the as yet unopened boutique by Zorah dressed in her grandmother's wedding
gown. Zorah's mother had been a sixties' flower child, and
now the daughter was following in her footsteps.

"The coffee's been ready for hours," Zorah whispered
hoarsely as he stood before her, his lips to her forehead. As
he kissed her, he remembered he hadn't brushed his teeth,
washed his face and hands, or written home, as he had
promised the Great Pacifier he would.

"Let me get washed up, Zee," he said in his deep basso,
"and then we'll have coffee, and then I'll finish laying the
floor tile, and then, if you'll be so kind, I'd love to fuck you."

"I can't stand it when you become so orderly," she
laughed.

He performed miracles with the equal but not separate
cooperation of Zorah, the wedding gown hiked up above her
fragile breasts, her willowy legs heel-locked behind his
white-as-snow skinny behind. She refused to let him go,
and, for the moment, he was satisfied with his condition.

"Mornings," he breathed into her ear, "are by far the best
times—a man has renewed energy after twenty-four hours
of sleeping and daydreaming."

Through teeth locked on his shoulder, she mumbled affir-
mation.

I'd like it, he thought, if she swallowed me whole, left
nothing, not a hair, not a drop of blood. Boy vanishes without a trace. He left me pregnant, weeps bride, patting
swollen belly. Inside her the vanished boy sleeps and swims
in eternal bliss, seeing her liquid world through a snorkler's
mask, Hawaiian sling on the alert for a floating kidney or a
spongy spleen. . . . No, no, I have to go . . . split . . . or as
the old man says in his quaint and ancient way, cop a beat,
jump the line . . .

Zorah felt him move, but held him tighter, his unshaven

chin bruising her smooth soft cheek. "Together maybe we can maybe make it till next week," she whispered.

"Let me go," he said, not moving, Zorah clutching him tighter.

If he had an escutcheon, she thought, that would be its legend. Let Me Go. He considered the slightest criticism an onslaught, the most faltering admonition a nagging lecture. He was as elusive as a ghost. She knew him now several months and thought she loved him. Did he love her? He never said, as if to say would be an admission of weakness. He laughed and made her laugh. He never posed and refused to permit her to pose. But he did pretend and refused to admit that he did. Now he relaxed into her embrace and she just loved the weight of him. Again he stirred and she said, "Don't move, please."

He lay on her quietly, and they could hear each other's breathing. Then from his own private space he said, "I have to find out for myself."

She recognized he was about to speak in one of his riddles. "Find out what?"

"I don't know—just find out. If I knew, I wouldn't have to find out."

"True, true," she said softly, moving her hips closer to him. "If I knew I wouldn't have to find out either."

"No one knows," he said. "My grandmother, my father, my mother, they don't know either, that's why they walk around so sad half the time. Everyone's looking. It seems they have it, but they don't. Always looking. For what? They don't know. I don't know. You don't know. Nobody knows. And it's probably right in front of our very own eyes. . . . Get closer,'" he whispered.

"Can't"

"Just try."

She tried.

"Ah, that's better." They were quiet a moment, then he resumed. "But they'll never find it. I'll never find it. Find what? Who knows? Let me alone, goddammit!"

"You're really going away?"

"Yes, I'm leaving."

She felt him withdraw. "Where are you going?"

"Texas, the Gulf of Mexico, California, Alaska, Australia. I don't know, and it doesn't matter anyway, does it? It's only a metaphor, isn't it?" He kissed her long white throat. "Going away, running away, seeing what's there instead of here, and when I'm there I'll want to be someplace else. It's all part of the same old deal. Looking."

She withdrew her hips, but he followed after her. They were silent, and again she felt him becoming hard. "How come," she asked, "you can be so smart and so dumb at the same time?"

"Who ain't?" he said. "Have you ever met anyone who's just stupid without being smart—and vice versa? The whole fucking world's stupid and smart simultaneously. The condition of man." And he grinned.

Zorah's legs and arms tightened about him. She bit his shoulder, rocked him gently, and he became hard as iron, plunging into her deeper and deeper, and Zorah rocked faster and faster and held him tighter, and again he thought, this time I'll disappear without a trace.

His lips found hers and their mouths sucked from each other, neither knowing whose lips bit whose and whose tongue was whose. Then they were quiet again. Her heels loosened their lock, her arms their hold. Advantage won, with a quick roll he slipped from her and was on his feet. He stared down at her, saw her lying there defeated, the wedding gown a shambles. He felt sad, but hardened his heart. No, I have to leave, have to do what I have to do. I promised her nothing.

———— 170 ————

"I'm leaving," he said softly.

"Good riddance."

"I'll be back."

"Don't do me any favors."

"It's not for forever."

"That's what the last one said."

Peter became infuriated. "Stop faking it, you're not giving an interview to a sociologist investigating the youth culture, the subculture, the counter-culture, the phony culture. We're not specimens." Just as swiftly he smiled gently, leaned over her, and helped her to her feet, and then smoothed the veil and tulle and satin about her. His eyes twinkled as they stared into hers, and he smiled tenderly. "You're very beautiful, Zorah."

She smiled tightly, her blue eyes sparkling with tears, her long black hair flowing to below her shoulders.

"You want me to do what you want," he said quietly, "and I want to do what I want."

She didn't answer, anger marking her face.

"I'll be seeing you," he said.

She merely stared at him, gritting her teeth, and bunching her lips.

"Goddamn you," he screamed, "I have to go, I don't know why, but I can't help it!"

Behind the slammed door, she stood coldly staring into space, as he vanished, left nothing, not a hair, not a drop of blood.

Pete Miller stood outside Needles at the juncture formed by the driveway of a Humpty-Dumpty Hamburg Hearth and the six-laner that ran straight as a rule through the Mojave

Desert to Barstow. The sun was as hot as a Bessemer furnace and if he didn't get a lift soon, air-conditioned, he hoped, he would burn down to a heap of red ash. Though face and head were protected by flaming red hair so he resembled a burning bush, his peeling nose jutted unsheltered. On his back was a rucksack containing *Fowler's Modern Usage*, a dictionary, a composition notebook, and brand-new black socks. On his feet his old Hush Puppies gasped openmouthed. His trousers were frayed, though moderately clean, his green polo shirt spotted with ketchup, mustard, and ice cream stains, some old, some fresh. He carried no sign—he didn't believe in it—it was too circumscribing, too definitive; he had no idea, after weeks on the road, where he was going, so why pretend or lie about it? Whoever gave him a hitch would take him as far as he or she was going, what made the difference where? Not that he hadn't had something in mind when he left New York how many weeks ago he could no longer remember; he had, but it had been vague, which he sometimes did pretend was a result of a conscious desire to be vague but which in his heart he knew was false. He had started out with the idea of retracing his father's footsteps—the South till Texas then up the Mississippi into the Midwest, Michigan, Illinois, Wisconsin, Iowa, Missouri and back again—but had given it up, had gone the way of his rides, and came to realize he was vague simply because he had no idea where he was going. He couldn't retrace his father's steps; it was impossible.

But he was on his own, that was one thing he had made up his mind about. Mom and Pop would have to get accustomed to the idea of it, as they would have to become accustomed to being alone again, just the two of them. They had their troubles, he knew, he wasn't blind, though perhaps they were. Some of the trouble was Pop, a lot of it was Mom, nearly every one-way street empties somewhere into a two-way avenue, otherwise not even a computer can determine the route to where you are going. What their trouble was was not for him to say, he had enough of his own, except for what was obvious. She was too damned easygoing, too calm, too sweet, and if she began giving back as much as she took—only half even—she would straighten the old man out, make him think before he did or said. As for his father, he was a little too quick on the trigger, old Tiger Max . . . he, Pete, had heard the story a million times. One thing was certain, they were neither of them uncomplicated, who was? That was a lesson he himself had learned the last couple of years and for that reason he wasn't making judgments. Strange about Mom and Pop—though the old man didn't conceal too much of himself, she concealed a real hardheaded anger behind her sweetness and light. But sometimes you couldn't help concealing what was going on inside, if for no other reason than that you were afraid of it. He understood that, too. Like when he'd been a coke snorter a few years ago. He hadn't wanted to snort coke; he had always liked his mind nice and clean. He despised drunks, he despised kids who tried to hide behind shit, so why should he be hiding even in the small way a coke snorter did? He wasn't making judgments, everyone had to decide for himself—or herself, he smiled—but still it was demeaning to hide, it was childish, it meant you were unable to overcome your fear. Like when he was afraid to come out into the open about not going to college. He'd suffered and hidden, afraid to tell his parents, and in the end made them suffer, too, because he'd led them to believe he was going. So he went for a year, made them spend all that money, wasted his time—got by without even trying, it was a snap—and at last screwed up the courage to tell them, "No more, I'm sorry," though he backtracked a bit, said I'll take the year off never really intending to return. If they hadn't got the point, they would now. College would never give him what he wanted or needed. He needed to experience his education, to feel it, to smell it, to see it, to ingest it through his pores. Then he was going to write it down, every word of it, each word his own, his style his own, so when he put it down it would be his, completely his. That was one thing he knew was definite. Nothing vague about that. He didn't need a professor telling him what Dostoevsky was driving at in every sentence of *The Brothers Karamazov* or Kafka in *The Castle*. He had his own brain, he could figure it out, especially since every professor understood it differently from every other, so that probably none of them knew what the hell they were talking about. There were a lot of kids going to college who were getting nothing out of it, so why go? Everyone made a goddamn fetish out of it. College was for Eli and Nina, his beloved siblings. Unlike them, he didn't talk easily; it took too much out of him, made him nervous, tense, trying to win the argument, top the professor, the other kid. It would have made a junkie out of him; he couldn't have gone through another year at school without turning on at every bend of the road. It was easier for him to talk to strangers on the street or on the road. They didn't challenge you—and if they did, hello and good-bye. He had to go his way on his own, alone. That was the only way he was happy. That was it, wasn't it? To be happy. If he didn't hurt anyone else, what was the harm in it? That was what his parents had taught him night and day all his life—try to avoid hurting other people as much as you can, it's almost impossible, but we have to try. He agreed. He didn't like to be hurt, and it was obvious no one else liked to be hurt. But it was a damn hard route. He hated hurting Mom and Pop, but they were parents and so had a built-in mechanism for being hurt by their children. He should have written them, but what the hell could he say that wouldn't hurt them? Perhaps he would write tonight, that is, if someone gave him a lift and he landed somewhere where he could write in his notebook.

Yeah, his notebook. So far he'd carried it three, four thousand miles and hadn't scribbled a word. Oh, well. He would write them something funny, make them laugh to ameliorate the pain. Like that time when he was fifteen and ran away. "Your fifteen-year-old son has reached that stage in life where Spock says he will run away. Don't worry." His father never tired of telling the story to friends. Everybody would laugh. Laughing helped. Generally when you laughed, you were laughing at someone. It is a release from fear of the person you are laughing at. He or she had made himself/herself—boy, they drove a man out of his mind with that he/she business—a little ridiculous and therefore not as dangerous as you thought he/she was or was afraid he/she was. A girl you like is cool and haughty. You do something funny. She laughs. You are not dangerous to her. She smiles at you. Soon you are in the sack, because since you've made yourself ridiculous you are no more powerful than she. He learned that early—very early. Make Mom and Pop laugh and they won't be pissed at you because you took the clock apart and couldn't put it together again. Humpty-Dumpty. Where's a lift?

The six-laner was a calamity of cars, and big trailer trucks roaring, farting, passing him by. If one car stalled there would be a pile up of twenty. Maniacs. Where were they going? They didn't know any more than he did. North or South, East, Southwest, big sprawling cities, rinkydink towns—rednecks, blacks, Indians, Chicanos, Vietnamese, Koreans, freaks, dudes, it didn't make any difference—they didn't most of them know where they were going. Food seemed to be plentiful, MacDonalds, Burger Kings, Humpty-Dumpties, Wimpies, Pig'n-a-Pokes, their garbage cans overflowing with food uneaten, wasted, enough to fill the stomachs of whole continents of despair. Bulldozers, houses, office buildings, hospitals, prisons, shopping centers going up, up, up, cars clogging the roads, roads choking off the woods, and everybody running, running, not knowing where the fuck they were going. Yet, he had to admit, most of them had been decent to him. It seemed only when they came in gangs, crowds, groups, sections, clans, cults that they became nasty and mean. You spoke politely. They spoke politely. They ripped you off. You ripped them off. You laughed. They laughed. Every prejudice, every stale piece of ignorance showed—but singly, or even in pairs, you spoke to them, they listened, they spoke to you, you listened, and they were decent and kind. He'd found them to be no less tolerant, even disagreeing violently with him, than any roomful of wiseass freaks in any dining room or loft in New York or Boston. They said they were Republican, you said you were Democrat, they argued, even got red in the face, but when they left you off, they wished you luck—if you're around here again, come call. One stiff-necked, redneck son-of-a-bitch had spouted his bonehead off about the niggers and kikes taking over the country, and when the guy took a breath, he, Pete, told him he was a Jew Democrat and the guy clammed up, almost stopped the car to throw him out, but then changed his mind, began to argue, shout, curse, but at the end of the ride, "So long, kid, hope you grow up soon." He smiled at the man, said, "Thanks for the ride, when the revolution comes I'll see we don't hang you," and the guy almost busted a gut laughing. But he certainly would hate to meet the guy when he was boozed up and backed by ten more like himself.

A red Buick showed its nose coming out of the Humpty-Dumpty driveway, and he raised his thumb. It was a girl, a beautiful head. He smiled. He could see her hesitating, so he moved fast towards the door, but she became frightened, stepped on the gas and took off like a shot. Jesus Christ, it was hot. Tonight he'd treat himself and go to a motel for a cold shower, maybe shave, cut off some of his hair, spruce up, eat a big meal. He still had two hundred fifty dollars left, was in good shape. You could hitch through this country on a dime. Easy rides, everyone asking if you were hungry, wanting to push food down your throat. The cars and trailers kept speeding past, the sun was a furnace. Lucky he'd freckled up, always had trouble with his light skin. The first few days his skin had become flag red, blistered, now only the damned nose never stopped peeling. Like a snake or a lizard, living under a flat stone to emerge at night to search out a bug or a bird's fallen egg, he liked cool dark places. Cars kept slamming past, whfff, whfff, rubber slapping blacktop. The orange sun soared high in the western sky. Fool, he'd picked the hottest day of the year to be in the Mojave Desert. Well, that was the luck of the draw when you hit the road, jumped the line, as his father used to say. Pop ran away at fifteen and didn't come home until he was more or less a man. "It was a lonely place"—still is, Pop— "but I ran into a guy named Ferrara, Angelo Ferrara, a real angel of life he was." Well, where was his, Peter's, angel of life? Right now in this bloody heat he would be a Godsend. Ha ha.

The truth was he needed no one. He was self-sufficient. Not even Zorah. She was a lovely girl, but she was too urgent, held on too tight, just what he didn't need at this stage of his life. He'd hurt her. Could he help it if she fell in love with him? He hadn't put himself out to make her. She'd put up a sign in her window saying she wanted a carpenter to put up some shelves, a painter to paint the walls, an electrician to run some wire for spotlights. So he applied for all of them and she hired him. He worked hard, did a good enough job, and he smiled at her. She smiled at him. He did a backflip. She laughed. He did a frontflip, stood on his hands, kissed her barefoot dirty toes. She made him stuffed grape leaves, which he hated, and bulgur, which he loved, and he bought a bottle of cheap Paisano wine, and they sat on pillows on the floor and feasted and drank while listening to the aging Stones drive the rats from the walls in a panic. They made love—but making it is not being it. Isn't that what the analyst told him when he went because sniffing coke was getting him down when he wanted to be up? He was sixteen and in trouble and his parents, blind as wooden ducks, couldn't figure out why. He felt sorry for them. Told them, "I'm a cokie, I need help." His mother cried, his father yelled, he thought the old bastard was going to have a heart attack. Not THEIR son. Why not? Was their son any different from all other sons and daughters in Kooch Behar-on-Hudson? On the Mississippi? On the Snake? Parents—blind as bats! Aaa, shit, he loved them. He wasn't going to whine like so many of his acquaintances that their parents didn't understand them, et cetera, et cetera, ad nauseum. A bunch of rip-offs, crybabies. Not him. He admired his parents, respected them, and loved them. Even his siblings, beloved siblings. There, you see, he was a good boy.

The blue nose of a Rabbit turned off the road to the shoulder ahead of him. A dude was driving. The Rabbit came to a halt. A big smile under dark sunglasses greeted him.

"Thanks," Pete said, "thought you'd never arrive, been waiting for you for hours."

The big smile laughed. Big, white shiny teeth in a tanned smooth face. Mustachios. Dressed like a fifties dude. Young. "Was held up by blue serge and shiny buttons. They searched my car, examined my tires, looked under my hood, front and rear—lucky I didn't fart—found nothing. I'm clean. They were polite. Where you going?"

"If you were black, they'd have ripped your ass open. . . . I don't know . . . as far as you'll take me, I suppose."

"Let me guess." Big-toothed smile. "You're from New York?"

"Right the first time," he said, belting himself in.

"Split from Mother and Father?"

"No. Just sightseeing, that's all."

The Rabbit hit seventy-five in ten seconds flat and was soon lost in traffic.

Pete sat belted into the baby blue Rabbit as Ronnie La-Motta, driving very fast through heavy traffic, talked and talked.

It was always his, Pete's, stupid luck to get locked in with people who talked without end. He must have listener engraved all over his face. They talked, he listened, suffered the fools their idiocies, was too fucking polite to ever tell them to, please, close their stupid holes. Several times, though, he'd been on the verge of telling the dude to shut his fucking lip and watch the scenery. They were ripping through the Mojave Desert, the sun was winging its way west towards the Pacific a few hundred miles away, and the red, yellow, and purple mesquite had a sheen of polished gold. Though the Rabbit was among the slowest cars on the road—even the double-humped semis were faster as they barrelled along on the desert flats—Ronnie had driven 73.4 miles in one hour and spoken one trillion words. None of them funny.

Pete Miller had listened to every one of them. All about cars. Ronnie LaMotta was a car buff, though he was going to college to become a lawyer so that his father, who was a contractor, wouldn't have to use lawyers outside the family. His father had to deal with racketeer unions and a man had to be careful or he would end up going to jail if the case came before the wrong judge. If you had the right judge, a decent, understanding merciful guy, you could make a contract and buy him off, but some of those guys were strict guardians of the law and sent you away, even knowing a contractor couldn't piss without paying off some union racketeer. That's the way it was, you know. His father gave him, Ronnie, more money than he knew what to do with because his father and mother had come from the old country and been piss poor, eating pasta all the time, and now, summanabitch, no kid of ours is going to starve, so he gave his boys three hundred baloneys a week to go to college and stay clean, keep away from the punks that gave Italians a bad name. His father was an honest businessman and he was going to be his lawyer to keep him out of the hands of those crummy union racketeers. (If Ronnie said that one more time, he, Pete Miller, was going to kick his teeth in.) The unions were ruining the country, everybody said that, you know, them and those welfare chiselers, then when a topnotch business needed money from the government because of some stupid government law everybody yelled their asshole heads off, especially those lefties at *The New York Times* and *The Wall Street Journal*. But Maseratis, that's what he loved. That was a car. Ferrari-Maserati, what a combo—makes the greatest music in the world. Can win any race, the Le Mans, the Daytona, the Indy. What he really wanted to be was a race car driver, drove his father out of his Wop head. You have to be a lawyer, his father said, have clean hands. No more dirty hands in this family. We made it big and we're gonna keep our LaMotta hands clean. No grease monkeys in his family.

Ronnie suffered from logorrhea, needed a mouth plug, kaopectate; he shit all over the place. Also drove too fucking fast. Made 37.2 miles in the next half hour in this little cockroach of a car that swerved everytime a truck passed it. One way Peter Miller didn't want to die was in a car accident. At least until he'd made up his mind about a couple of things. The six-laner ran straight and flat through the desert, the mesquite glittering gold and lavender when the traffic didn't get in the way.

Pete wanted to tell Ronnie to slow it down, this piece of tin wasn't really good enough on the road to continue going at this pace. But what the hell, Ronnie seemed to be a very good driver, knew what he was doing, let it go, the hell with it. Pete also wanted to stop Ronnie from talking, wanted to challenge some of his assertions, make some of his own, especially about unions. He knew plenty about unions and honest porkchoppers, but what was the use of interrupting the dude; no matter what he, Pete, said, Ronnie would still go on believing or at least saying the things he did, because he probably didn't believe anything. So far as Pete could remember, no one ever changed his mind about his beliefs because of what someone else said. Ronnie might well say, I suppose so, maybe you're right, yeah, that's true, and then turn around and say the same old shit again. Besides, he, Pete, would have to break through that flow of words, and it took more energy than he seemed to have. He was tired, had been on the road for weeks, was approaching California where he would do what? Nothing. Anyway, if Ronnie had a brain in his head, he'd begin to learn the difference between bullshit and truth before his life was over. If he didn't, then it didn't matter anyway.

So Pete didn't interrupt Ronnie and Ronnie didn't stop talking. They passed a sign which said Barstow 40 miles. When Ronnie had stopped to give him a lift outside Needles, and asked where he was going, he'd answered as far as you're going, which of course meant nowhere. But he'd never asked Ronnie where he was going.

Pete waited for Ronnie to take a breath, then rushed in with the words, "Where you going, Ronnie?" He did want to know where he was going to sleep that night.

Ronnie hesitated a moment, finally at a loss for words. Pete observed him. Ronnie was biting his lips, chewing on the big droopy black mustache of an old wild west bandito which circumscribed the lush curve of his mouth. His shoulders were hunched over the wheel of the little car, and his dark eyes stared straight ahead, his eyebrows expressively raised at some question he was asking himself. Ronnie had a friendly, generous face, intelligent, too, and had run off at the mouth repeating the same old shit he'd heard all his life. Hardly any different from himself, Pete Miller, who also repeated most of the things he'd heard all his life. They were separated only by circumstances. If Ronnie had been born a Miller he would be saying or thinking the things Pete thought or said—when he finally said—and vice versa. Ronnie was cogitating very deeply, quiet now, the car going faster than it had before, hitting close to eighty, yet being passed by trucks and cars going ninety. There wasn't a trooper in sight. Pete wondered why Ronnie was taking so long to answer his simple question. Surely, Ronnie LaMotta who received three hundred baloneys a week from his old man just to go to school knew where he was going. He saw that Ronnie had at last come to some decision and was now ready to speak.

"You know, Petey, I don't know where I'm going."

"Don't call me Petey. What do you mean?"

"You asked me where I was going, right?"

"Right."

"I don't know. I was going to Barstow to visit some cousins, but I don't want to go to Barstow. I don't know where I'm going."

"Go ahead, I'm listening."

"You're a good listener, Petey, I was—"

"I said don't call me Petey."

"Sorry. I was shooting off at the mouth and you never interrupted me once. You know?"

"I know what you mean. That's what I'm known for best—listening."

"You, too?"

Pete laughed. "If you're a listener, you never for a second

let me see it. You talked for an hour and a half straight. In fact, for 103.6 miles."

Ronnie shrugged his shoulders. "You got the kind of face that says you're a listener. You know? When I asked you where you were going and you said as far as you'll take me, I thought, Jesus, this freak's free and here I'm doing everything I don't want to do. I don't want to be a lawyer for the old man. If I'm his lawyer I'll be his little boy Ronnie for the rest of my life. Even after he's dead. I don't wanna be his little boy. I wanna be Ronnie LaMotta all by himself. . . . Listen, ain't there *any* particular place you're going?"

"No, I told you the truth. I'm just going wherever the rides take me."

"What if I said I'm gonna turn around at the next exit and go to Santa Fe?"

"Why not? I was near there a couple days ago and didn't drop in, even though it's a place I always wanted to see. Just love the sound of the name. Santa Fe. New Mexico. Piss poor Indians, Chicanos, squaws weaving baskets in the streets, white adobe huts, squalid hogans, half the people talking Spanish, half English. I'd just love to turn around and go to Santa Fe."

Ronnie laughed, looked at him quickly with a joke in his eye. "Okay, let's go to Denver."

"The continental divide. Towering mountains. Snow. Crossroads to the West. Ugly metropolis in the midst of splendor. Highest incidence of crime in the United States. A plane every minute. The Rockies. Wildcats. Cougars. Rugged men and whiteskinned women wearing fashions two years out of date. Big business. Durango. Boulder. Estes Park. Sure, let's go to Denver."

"For a listener, you do pretty good, Pete."

Shyly. "Yeah, once I get started I'm pretty hard to stop. Just like you."

With a laugh Ronnie slapped at the wheel, the car

swerved, and he caught it. "Say, let's go on the bum together."

Pete stared at him in astonishment, then smiled. "On the bum? How much bread do you have stashed in those slick duds of yours?"

"Two hundred fifty in cash, an AmeriBank credit card and my checkbook."

"How much in your checking account?"

"A couple thousand. Hey, why? You flat?"

"No. I started out from New York a few weeks ago with over four hundred. Transportation free, slept in cars or camped out, a rare cheap motel, pizzas, hamburgers, hominy grits, submarines, hoagies, wedgies, coca cola. Still got more than half—a good deal more than half. . . . We can't go on the bum, kid, just can't."

"Why not? You said you were going nowhere. Ain't that being on the bum?"

"It could be. But then we'd be the richest bums in America. The Aging Bull, that is, my father, once told me you can't be on the bum unless you don't know where your next crumb's coming from, otherwise you're just pretending, it's a fake." Pete saw that Ronnie looked disappointed, the kid liked the idea of being on the bum. "If you have money in your jeans and you're on the road to nowhere, it's not being on the bum, it's being lost. So let's be accurate and not sentimental about it because sentimentality's cheap, like buying a cheap cry, do you know what I mean?"

"Yes. You get all excited over a Jaguar, it looks so classy, a fantastic car, but then you buy one and find out it's a piece of junk lying in the repair shop all the time, so you keep it parked in front of the house and get a cheap thrill out of it when someone says wow, what a car, when you know inside it's a piece of crap."

"So let's not be sentimental. Let's call it what it is. Let's call it running away together."

"It won't sound so good when we come back and tell everybody about it."

"When you run away, you don't think of going back, at least I don't think so. I haven't thought once today of what it would be like going back."

"Maybe that's because you've been thinking about running away longer than me. I'll get around to it. I'm a fast learner. At college one of my professors said I had absolutely no aptitude for the legal profession but that I was a good learner and would manage. I think he was ripping me off; I wouldn't make a good lawyer in a million years. My brother Louie's the one who'd make a good lawyer. Has lots of rocket power. I think I'm built for running away."

They were quiet. They passed a slowing truck and the Rabbit swerved sharply and Ronnie had to hold on hard.

"That's the only bug in this baby carriage. If they put front wheel drive in and made it a little lower, it would hold the road better."

"But then it would be a different car. If you and I had a little rocket power up our asses, we wouldn't be running away, and we wouldn't be Ronnie and Pete, we'd be Louie and Eli. Eli's my brother; he and my sister Nina are the ones with rocket power in my family. I'm the one who's still being powered by an old piston engine."

Ronnie laughed.

Dusk purpled the sky. Lights began to make their appearance up ahead in a chaotic pattern, like the slow haphazard emergence of stars. Another half hour had passed and they'd gone another 35.7 miles. Barstow was fast approaching, signaled by a shimmering yellow glow in the sky.

Peter rested easy. Ronnie would probably cop out when they hit Barstow. The thought was comforting. Having a brand new Rabbit at his disposal would lessen the excitement of erratic incident, make it too comfortable, besides he hated to have to defer to another's wishes. He didn't want to impose his own vagarious impulses on Ronnie and vice versa. Another person made it complicated and complication was what he'd run away from. He wanted to coast along at his own speed, hiding in silence when he wanted to, not having to listen when he didn't want to. Now he'd have to worry about hurting Ronnie's feelings. People, goddamn it, never let you alone.

Cars and trucks were passing them left and right. What the hell was Ronnie driving in the middle lane for, why didn't he move his ass over? The middle lane was the one where you could most easily be clobbered. Dumb son of a bitch. The story of his life, being caught in the middle. He'd have to ditch Ronnie, his feelings be damned. Why had it been Ronnie who'd stopped, not another? There was nothing in this ripoff of a world you could be sure of. Your parents were like everybody else's—tired, in a panic, dying to touch solid bottom with their toes after a long swim. Soon they would be in an old-age home like Nanny Ruth. Would he some day? What an ignominious way to end your life—with a bunch of wretched old people, sick, moaning, crying, dying. Was Nanny Miriam's way better? Dad had taken her to an old-age home and she ran away. Not me, she snapped, I'm going to die in my own bed. She became sick and almost did. Dad had to take her in his arms, carry her out of her apartment, put her in the car and drive her to the hospital. She screamed, she howled, called Dad every name she could think of, and died. Dad was so mad at her he didn't cry for a month. Then one morning, he locked himself in his room and wouldn't come out. Mom said he was crying. He sat in that room for seven days. Pop didn't pray, but he was mourning for his mother.

A huge tractor-trailer passed them on the right hitting eighty-five. The car swung wildly to the left and Peter instinctively moved to grab the wheel but the seat belt held him. Ronnie straightened her out, then turned to him and laughed.

"Mr. LaMotta, you're just hellbent for destruction."
Ronnie laughed again.
They were soon in Barstow and said their good-byes.
"Thanks for the ride."
"Yeah, be seeing you."

Dear Mother and Father,

I'm writing from Xanadu where I still am and will possibly remain for a number of weeks, most likely until the end of September. I decided to stay for a number of reasons. Xanadu isn't too bad a town. The city itself is fairly ugly and has little to recommend it, but the environs are truly beautiful. Mountains surround Xanadu on most sides, the falls prominent on the skyline and Mt. Dorado standing alone and snow-covered are very close on a clear day. There's the true wilderness less than an hour's drive from town in one direction and the Pacific as near in the other. Much more violent than the Atlantic, with strangely shaped grotesquely towering rocks just off the shore. Unfortunately the water's too cold to swim in, and anyway I have a fine layer of dirt on my body which I've worked years to preserve. I haven't been staying with King Dahfu and his lion but with a very nice young woman who—whom I met about a week after I arrived. A rather remarkable girl with a fine intelligence, educated and literate, an excellent companion and just incidentally she can cook damned good and she's very beautiful to boot. Splendid teeth. She says I'm a throwback and why (1) don't I go to work? or (2) return to college? The relationship unfortunately is only temporary.

Greetings to my brother and sister.

Love,
Pete

Dear Peter,

As soon as I saw your scribbled hand peeking out from among the mail I became exceedingly happy because I knew you were happy. Then I read your letter and was doubly happy. Especially that you were living with a remarkable, intelligent, literate girl who can cook. Splendid teeth. But I'm very curious about how you know in advance that a relationship is only temporary. When you met her, did the girl wear a sign which read: For Temporary Use Only? Or was it you who bore a sign: Beware! I Am Temporary? It intrigues me. Please let me know. Dad sends his love. Me, too.

Mom

Dear Mother,

Xanadu turned out to be fake. I hitched and got a ride with an Indian. Sad-faced, laconic brave. He said he would show me a place I've never seen. But first he had to blindfold me. He looked benign enough, and besides he was a Ph.D.—the highest form of life on earth—so I said okay. We drove all day and all night. (Don't worry, Mom, we stopped to eat and do the necessaries.) In the morning he took the blindfold from my blinking eyes. It was Shangrila. It was even uglier than Xanadu with high cornflake box buildings and a fake Greek cultural center with marble toothpick columns and very busy with all sorts of people running madly around. I thought they were rather amusing because they pretended they were different from everybody else. Shangrila is surrounded by huge pine forests and ice cold lakes which glimmer like dark mirrors under the moonlight. I have decided to stay a while. I still

haven't washed and my toes stick out of my socks. Today
I think I will buy a new pair if I get around to it. Love to
the Aging Bull and to my beloved siblings.

Your son,
Pete

Dear Peter,
    You can get it at a newsstand for a quarter.

Love,
Mom

Dear Mom,
    Only got a dime.

Pete

Dear Peter,
    Tough.

Mom

NINA—4

Dearest Mom,

This will be short because I've got to mail it today and
I'm not in a writing mood. Mom, this is just between you
and I—oops! I'm sorry, Mom. I'm trying to remember
that prepositions take the objective, but it's very hard to
remember because everybody, but everybody, including
television announcers says between you and I. Anyway,
this is just between you and me. It's something I don't
feel I can discuss with Dad. I'm having this trouble—well,
I guess about sex. It pisses me off, it really does. What do
the boys think I am? Because I'm friendly, easygoing, they
treat me like I'm—I don't know how to say it, I'm just so
mad. They don't seem to understand that I don't want to
trade my body just so I can say I've got a boy friend. Big
deal! What a nerve! What assholes! Maybe *they* can separate their body from their minds and feelings, but my
body's got feelings and isn't my brain part of it? As soon
as we sit down and talk they want to hold hands. That's
fine with me. It's pleasant. But that's the first mistake,
too. The next thing you know they're running their fingers up my legs, you know, like pretending I don't know
they're doing it. I'm talking about something important
like my feelings and things like that and they pretend to
be very interested—but they're really interested in only
one thing. I like my body. It's not bad-looking and I love
to decorate it with different sorts of clothes. They think I
decorate it for them, the pissasses. Maybe I do a little bit,
but I think I do it for myself mostly. But no matter what,

they're always trying to get into my clothes, damn them, and into me with their scruffy hands. I admit I like their bodies, too, but mostly I like them when they are interesting and interested in what I have to say. I get so bored with having to make out all the time! Christ! Was Daddy like that when he was young? Puff puff, huff huff, woof woof. They have to be touching all the time, for God's sake! It's not that I'm a prude or an iceberg. I like to kiss, I like to hug, I like to make out, too, but I like the good feeling of talking and trying to understand each other—you know what I mean, Mom?

And then the one I told you about that I really like—Michael—you remember him?—well, lately he's been drinking beer whenever he gets a chance. Ugh! Phew! Does he stink when he drinks. All the boys do. That really makes me want to puke. He's slobbering over me, saying those stupid things and trying to hug me, and I crack up and I can't stop giggling because all I can think of is green olives. That's how he smells. I giggled so much the poor guy got insulted.

Mom, it's good to be able to write to you about this stuff. It makes me sad when I remember what you told me about you and your sisters not having anyone to talk to when you were kids—not even to each other. It must have been terrible. Don't let what I've written worry you, though, I guess it'll work out okay someday when I meet that great RIGHT ONE. (Ha, ha.)

I can't wait for you to come up soon. I hope Dad's with you. Lots of kisses, Momsie, and don't forget this is between you and I.

Love and xxxxxx
Nina

P.S. I did meet a new guy. Richard the Lionhearted. Oh boy!

N.

ROUND AND ROUND

She and Max were strolling through the woods near the lake cottage. The children were off, rowing or fishing, perhaps hiking, and she was speaking to him but as usual he wasn't listening, didn't seem to hear a word, was oblivious, involved with his inner life, perhaps seeing his black and white movie, and she ran off under the trees, hoping he would follow after her. In a few minutes she stopped to listen for his footsteps, but there were none.

The woods were cool, speckled with sun filtering through the leaves and pine needles, not a whisper, not even a cicada calling, and she became suddenly frightened and started back on the same path but was soon lost. The sun—where was the sun? Ah, there it was, hidden behind some clouds. She calmed her frantic nerves by counting one, two, three, four, slowed her breathing. Behind her a forest animal stirred, skittered swiftly into the underbrush and she stood rigidly, her chest constricted, her hands shaking, her vocal chords paralyzed with fear. Max merely stared, his grin frozen, only the sun alive in his glass eye. She could hear herself moaning, the silence about them shattered by the screeching of birds. She tore loose, the birds screaming at her, the sun blinding her, yet its warmth a pleasant caress on her naked arms. She raised one hand to shield her eyes, turned back again to Max, but of course he wasn't there— he'd left early that morning. She was in their big bed—it had been a dream. The house was silent except for the cheery chirp of a nuthatch as it airily tripped head first down the trunk of the maple tree outside the window and for the angry screams of a grackle couple as they dueled with the neighbor's cat. She hoped the cat would shoot them down with outflung claw.

Rebecca sat up, controlled her breathing, one, two, three, four, then closed her eyes, sighing sorrowfully, and recognized the sharp bite of unhappiness in her stomach. Dozed. Woke. Dozed. Round and round, the grand sugar maples and tall pines swaying high above her, she skated on the secondhand ice skates Shep Nielson had given her. She was euphoric. She was Sonja Henie. She won the national figure skating championship . . . went on to the Olympics . . . received the gold medal to the plaudits of thousands as "The Star-Spangled Banner" played. Under her breath she sang the "International" . . . she'd won for the wretched of the earth . . . for Papa. Round and round the little pond, the other kids forgotten, unseen, the majestic sugar maples singing in the wind, snowflakes falling, the tall pines piercing the blue sky. Without a word Dominic Eboli joined her, took her mittened hands in his, and together, silently, they whirled round and round the little pond. As evening approached, they dropped hands, parted, and still silently, without a word, went their separate ways through the woods. She glowed. She was in love for the first time ever.

The following afternoon, again, his hands and hers clasped tightly, round and round, silently, without a word, they glided, their bodies one, their hearts fused, round and round the little pond, the sugar maples powdered with snow and the pine needles glistening, their faces glowing, at the end of her nose a tiny icicle. And again, as the sun plumetted behind the trees, a ball of gold, they dropped hands, parted, and still silently, without a word, wound their separate ways home. She glowed. She was in love. He was a senior at Springfield High, she a lowly sophomore; they were both so shy. She burned with love. Had a terrible fever . . . red splotches covered her entire body. She had the measles. Her silent lover would pass her in school that spring, never speak a word. In June he graduated and she never saw him again.

Her head plunged deep in the pillow, Rebecca drew the linen coverlet over her quivering body. Dominic Eboli, a handsome, dark boy. My God, how she had just wanted to hold hands with him—that was all, just hold hands. Unfinished business, one went through life with so much unfinished business. She dozed again. Awoke. Listened for house noises. Looked at the clock. 7:00—her habitual waking hour—waited to hear beds creak, doors slam, the toilet flush, the faucets gush. Nothing, they were all gone.

It was just about a month since Max and she had driven Nina to prep school—preparatory school for an Elias and a Miller, from rags to Saks Fifth Avenue in one generation, only in America, as Max's mother used to say—installed her in her room, met her roommates, kissed, hugged, gave last minute instructions, admonishments, "Yes, Mom; sure, Pops," and left her behind, the third of their three children.

Today, at dawn, Max rode off to North Carolina on union business. "I'll be back as soon's I can," he said after a hurried peck, and she almost, but hadn't, said, "Take your blasted time, no hurry." As he backed out the driveway she could see that he was already seeing his homemade movie, unreeling his past and his present, oblivious to the world. She hoped he wouldn't forget himself one of these days and end up plastered against an overpass abutment. Hoped.

Langorously, lonesomely, she stretched. If only Max were next to her now, waking with a smile, his empty eye socket pinched tight, his good brown eye measuring. "C'mere, hon, wanna nibble on 'at 'ig tit." Not until he washed and had his coffee did he begin to articulate words sharply. Max Miller, roughhewn hero of *Max, a Black and White Movie*.

Rebecca smiled ruefully to herself. It was true. When he daydreamed of the past, it was always in movie form, himself the hero—like when he did that oral history a few months ago, wasn't he the big hero then—but fully awake he was very much in the present. She curled, knees to soft belly, under the coverlet and closed her eyes. Now that he was gone, she missed him, wanted to unveil her soul to him, spill the beans about herself. Yet, when he was present, after some twenty-five years, there wasn't that much to say, not recently anyway. And she'd always found it difficult to speak about intimate things to anyone, even Max. In the early days of their marriage it used to upset him. He'd cajole, urge, yell, admonish, then give up. "Okay, Mrs. Pokerface, keep your goddamn thoughts to yourself." Though it never prevented him from emptying his own bag of thoughts on the kitchen table before her. Then, suddenly, in the last six months or so he'd given that up, too. It didn't take too much to send him off on his daydreams, fantasies, inventions. She could hardly blame him, even though he'd begun to shut out the children, too. Now that he was gone, blast it, she wanted to talk with him, to discuss their lives, her vague unhappiness, the terrible lonesomeness in a house empty of children, her work at the day care center, the biting hunger (not so secret wants and desires) which rattled the rib cage surrounding her heart. If she spoke to him, perhaps it would help her understand, help her delineate exactly what that hunger was—a hunger that seemed so easy to satisfy, yet when seemingly satisfied not satisfied at all. She was gliding round and round on that little pond. How could she possibly discuss with Max what she was afraid or unable to discuss with herself? If only she could do what he did—replay the past the better to understand the present. How easy it seemed to him. Was it really?

She remembered the previous night. Max and she sat on the sofa in the living room. The house was quiet. Max read a book as she knitted a sweater for him. As the needles darted and pulled she began to daydream of her youth in Springfield when her father was still alive and sitting at the kitchen table, drinking hot tea, reading a newspaper and singing softly to himself, as Ma ironed clothes near the red hot black coal stove. One of the pleasanter evenings, when Pa stayed home instead of running off to meetings or his whore-mongering. She could hear the song Pa was singing, a Russian song about two young men picking up two girls and going for a drive in an open *droshky* along the Neva in St. Petersburg. Now she herself began to hum it softly to herself.

Her voice was low, an alto. Inwardly smiling, she noticed from a corner of her eye the book fall shut on Max's knees. He closed his eyes, a faint bemused smile curled his lips, his scarred, rough face softening. He was, she knew, viewing a scene from his movie (a stab at survival—this is me, this is how I've lived). It was the same scene, she was certain, he saw every time she sang softly in his presence.

When she stopped humming, Max turned to her, his good eye open now, the eyelid of his bad drooping, and she stopped knitting so she could face him. The bemused smile faded from his lips, and a sadness hovered about his face, a sadness softened by the years, patinaed with the experiences of his life. Then he said, "The sky opened up and the shit and the piss poured down until we were almost drowned alive in it. . . . Oh, Christ, why'd you get me started on it? People who are nostalgic for the thirties don't know nothing—anything about them or didn't live through them. You know even though you were a little kid . . ." And he picked up his book again, but she didn't want him to read, to leave her, so she asked him, not knowing why in the world she did:

"Do you still love me, Max?"

"Hell, no," he smiled, "I just live with you because I'm too lazy to find another woman."

She resumed knitting, her eyes on the long needles, but she knew he continued to observe her, and she was sorry she'd begun what she didn't want to finish.

"What's the matter, Becky—what's ailing you?"

She didn't answer. She couldn't possibly tell him what she had on her mind.

"There you go again," he said sharply. "First you start it, then you clam up. Aren't you aware that that's what you do?"

The long needles stabbed, her eyes following their passage, her mouth shut tight. Yes, she was aware of it, of course she was.

"You feeling bad because the kids are all gone and I have to leave for a couple of weeks?"

She couldn't refuse to speak, especially since she *had* started it. "I suppose so. It's the first time in about twenty-five years that I'll be totally alone."

"Are you implying that I shouldn't go?"

"Of course not, I know you have to."

"It wasn't my idea that Nina go to private school."

"Mine either. But we could hardly say no to her when she wanted so much to go and they gave her a scholarship for it."

"So you'll be lonesome. It won't be the first time."

"Yes, I'll be lonesome." Wanted to say more, stopped. Perhaps she ought to speak to him about it, have it out. Have what out? Besides, she'd always wanted some solitude, her own time—time for myself, how many times had she thought it or talked about it with her women friends?—so what was she complaining about?

He tried, though, poor man, he tried. "You returned to work, have a job in a day care center, something you've always wanted to do. I got my job, it's not as if we're both ready to retire and die, especially you, you're a good four-teen, fifteen years younger than I am. . . . I get lonesome, too, when I'm away, you know that, don't you?"

"Forget it, Max. I have a right to feel low after my young-est child's gone, left home, vamoosed, couldn't wait to get away, and my husband's going off to fight the dragons again, though it is much safer in the South than it used to be."

He grabbed her hands roughly. "Look at me, damn you!"

Angrily she stuffed the half-knitted sweater, needles and yarn into the red canvas bag she used, then lifted her eyes to his face. His teeth were clenched tight and his good eye glared. Cyclops. Tiger Max. Go ahead, tell him, what in the world are you afraid of? "Perhaps it's good you're going away . . . will give us both time to sift out our emotions . . . come to some understanding about how we're going to live without children—just the two of us again."

"Stop bullshitting me, will you, that's not what's on your mind. Besides, we'll live the way we've always lived. The kids haven't gone away to some new world never to be seen again like our parents did. Even Pete, the little bastard, he always manages to stay in touch. And though Eli and I still have big fights whenever he's home, we love each other, and he's nuts about you, too nuts about you if you ask me. So what the hell's there to think about or worry about?"

She shrugged. He was a pragmatist. One did what one had to do. "You're life's hardly affected by Nina's going away. Mine is deeply affected. I've had children to feed, dress, coddle, even decipher for twenty-four years. All of a sudden there's a void."

"Some void. Stop bleeding. You have a job now, friends, a full life—what the hell else d'you want?"

Everything, she wanted to say. "Nothing, Max, nothing at all. Let's go to sleep. You have to get up early, you have a long drive." She'd had her chance, now she'd given it up. If she had opened herself to him, he would have helped her; he always had even if it hurt him, pragmatic realist that he was. She began to rise and he made a move as if to grab her arm, to stop her by force, but he gave up, too.

As she was almost out of the room, he called after her, and she stopped to look back at him. He spoke almost through clenched teeth. "You know, Rebecca, I'm sick and tired—can hardly take any more of it—this wall, a new wall now, that you've begun to build between us. Suddenly it's getting higher. We won't be able to see each other's eyes soon. If you have something to say to me, say it. You start, you stop—you got me on the edge of the roof. If I'm not good enough for you to talk to anymore, then tell me and after all these years I'll go peddle my fish someplace else. I've really had enough of it. You hold it in—pain, worry, unhappiness. I don't know what it is—as if you love it, can't stand to give it up. No wonder I keep going off into myself. What should I do—look at you waiting for the word?" His face was white, angry, pained, frustrated.

She could feel his pain and stepped towards him, wanted to speak out to him, cry out, why not, he was her husband, he loved her, she loved him, but there it was, she couldn't. Some sort of idiot pride prevented her, a self-made stricture against crying out, a fear it would sound as if she were pleading for herself—she didn't exactly know, did she? Mama, Mama, if only you could help me? Mama, I love you so much. . . . Max kept looking at her and she knew if she just said to him, "Max, I love you, I wish I could tell you what it is, but I can't because I just don't know myself," he would accept that and jump to his feet and take her in his arms, forgive her for the thousandth time. But she could give him nothing but a cold stare, an immobile mouth. Mrs. Pokerface. Suddenly with sort of a controlled fury, he said, "Go take a flying fuck for yourself!" and marched out to the screened-in porch that adjoined the living room.

Mrs. Pokerface marched upstairs, prepared for bed, waited for him, but he didn't come up and she soon fell asleep. Her ability to fall asleep no matter what was both her salvation and her damnation. She herself marveled at how easily sleep enfolded her in its arms under even the most dire of circumstances—and it did again. She didn't even hear Max when he slipped into bed sometime later, though she did in her sleep feel him conforming his body to hers, cupping her breast in his large hand, and remembered sleepily hoping he'd turn her on her back. He didn't—sleep intervened. When he woke before dawn, she woke, too, and went down and made him some breakfast, and then walked out to the car with him. He was, she knew, again waiting for her to say some word to him, but she couldn't. She could practically hear him sigh with relief when he slid behind the steering wheel and the car door closed behind him. As she stood observing him back out of the driveway, he was already fading her out, staring into his past.

Lips tight, step heavy, she returned to bed, began to think about their quarrel—quarrel? You can't quarrel with hemstitched lips. Oh, Becky, you fool, you fool. . . . She fell asleep again, and dreamt dreams which replicated reality.

Now Max was gone, the tangy smell of him still lingering in the bed. His section of the closet was tidy and shut, his dresser drawers closed—no trace of him. He raised cleanliness and neatness to the point of fetish. Her section of the closet was wide open, two drawers of her bureau slightly agape, a pair of mauve pantyhose sticking out like a sickly red tongue, the clothes she'd worn the night before draped over a chair. Max had given up bothering her about that, too, had learned to accept her simple, normal lack of fastidiousness after many years. "Funny thing about you, Beck, that's the only way you ever expose yourself."

She fought against returning to the escape of sleep and with abrupt decision leaped from the bed.

Rebecca Miller—a tall, full-figured energetic middle-aged woman. Suffers neither from constipation nor from sluggish arteries. Usually knows what she wants and steadfastly goes after it. Customarily delights her family and friends with her calm nature and gentle wit. Now she's momentarily unhappy. Poor thing.

Behind her, the mauve-tongued mouth of the bureau laughed at her.

Showered, dressed in vivid colors—crimson pants over big rump, purple sleeveless turtleneck jersey over soft breasts shaped round by bra (not a bad-looking head, as Max Miller, husband, would say)—Rebecca gazed about the bedroom one more time. Bed unmade, dresser drawers ajar and overflowing, her closet doors wide open. To hell with it, she didn't have to do a blasted thing. Her time was her own, her life was her own, she belonged to nobody. Up theirs! Yours, too, Max Miller! She grinned into the mirror, then sauntered down to the kitchen bathed by the same brilliant early September sun, breakfasted on cold orange juice, wholewheat toast, marmalade, a cup of steaming hot coffee, very strong and black. Then, her two feet up on Max's chair, another cup of hot coffee, the *Times* open before her, she killed a good hour. Suddenly swept cup, saucer, plates, utensils, newspaper to the floor. Leaped to her feet. Stared in anguish about her. The house, empty, seemed huge, hollow. The stillness was almost frightening. She kept staring at the electric clock on the kitchen wall. It barely seemed to move. She heard the birds twittering, an occasional car in the street, a dog bark, and for some unearthly reason felt like a prisoner behind bars.

Finally, she roused herself. Hurriedly cleaned the mess from the floor—four, five dollars worth of dishes, damn!—set the house in order. Banged in her dresser drawers, tidied her closet, shut its sliding doors with a slam, wrestled the big double bed into shape. Stared at the clock on the bed table. No matter what, like some damned robot she was always right on time. Ten o'clock. At eleven she would call her mother at the old-age home. At 12:30 she would leave for her job. She couldn't wait to hear the four-year olds chirping, crying, howling and Mrs. Gedney's officious lectures on child rearing and education. Thought of calling

Alice Peerce or Liz Morrison to make a date for lunch tomorrow. So soon? Was this the way it was going to be after waiting long, impatient years for some needed solitude? For good, solid soul-searching? She wished her mother was still living with them. Mama, Mama—the thought of her mother brought with it sadness, a sadness that for many years she'd forgotten, buried deep, and that had abruptly in recent weeks returned to shadow her life.

To pass the time, she sat in the screened-in porch knitting needles in hand, the sun, fragmented by mountain laurel and large ancient blue spruce trees, splashing over her shoulders.

The Golden Lady, that's what Liz Morrison's husband called Becky. He was referring to her smile and to her coloration, especially since her graying red hair, transformed by the alchemy of the summer sun, became a radiant gold. To him, at least, she lit up the room. Perhaps that was because his own wife had a sallow complexion and was brilliantly witty at his expense, sharp-tongued. Rebecca was easy-going, backed away from quarrels. Most quarrels were silly, childish. Other friends referred to her as mature, meaning reasonable, measured, rarely if ever sharply critical of them. Becky, she's a brick. You needed some advice about your kids, why, call Becky Miller, after all that's her field. She was marvelous with children, not so much because she loved them, which she did, but because she seemed to understand them even when they were most obtuse. Brats stopped acting bratty after being around her for a while.

There were other people who thought Rebecca Miller cool, haughty, not overly friendly, perhaps a snob. She didn't make a great effort to be friendly, perhaps she was a snob. If she didn't like you, she had little to do with you, made no effort at all to put herself out. It had nothing to do with the fact that she was extremely well read. The nineteenth was Rebecca's century—in literature as well as in personal behavior. She preferred Jane Austen to Erotica Gong. Becky's old-fashioned, Liz Morrison, an old friend, always said. Sane. Reasonable. Mature. Liz made it sound as if Becky suffered from some disease; that it was more interesting to be as neurotic, as unreasonable as she, ass-swiveling, unable to sit in one spot very long, always plucking at some man's sleeve. She thought Becky was as comfortable as an old sofa, its gold upholstery still radiant, a little worn perhaps. But many men thought it might be lovely to be enfolded in Rebecca's comfortable arms, though she gave them very little if any come hither, yet none ever made a move. Perhaps they were afraid of Max. If you got a little too close to his wife, Max Miller just shoved you aside— gently, but with unmistakable meaning. Though in his sixties, Max was still brawny, and his fists like cannonballs.

Rebecca's children had an easy time with their mother. Peter called her the Great Pacifier, meaning she both kept you calm and that she could not endure fights in the house. If anything upset her, it was fighting. She insisted on peace. Nina called her the Laughing Lady. Mom, don't you ever get mad? You're always laughing. It wasn't true that she was Mrs. Pokerface, though she did keep to a certain reserve, wasn't always hugging and loudly proclaiming her love. Yet no one in her family ever for a moment doubted that love. If anything troubled Becky, she became exceedingly quiet, rarely spoke. Max would scream, rage, rant, to no avail. He was fifteen years her senior. My child bride. He was getting on, but so was she, though at a slower pace.

Eli, Rebecca's eldest, thought he knew his mother best of all. Eli was a painter, or at least at twenty-four hoped to be. He observed his mother very carefully, then he painted her portrait and it turned out to be a copy of Parmigianino's

Lady with a Long Neck that his professor had analyzed in art history class. He returned to the model, again observed her closely, this time sketched her, returned to his studio apartment in Manhattan, spent endless hours on his canvas, this time it turned out to be a copy of Courbet's voluptuous nude rising from the sea which hung at the Met. Still, still, he thought he was getting closer. Eli knew his mother was not a laughing lady, not a soft touch, not as serene as everyone said. His mother's fingernails were bitten to the quick, and the right corner of her lower lip was scarred from having been kneaded by her teeth so often. No, no, his mother was not without her inner agony.

Max knew that, too. Also knew she was stubborn, stubborn and even ferocious when it came to her cubs, those at home and those at the day care center. Liz Morrison went back to college after her children became school age and received her degree in child care. Anything Rebecca Miller could do, Liz could do better. Just recently when an opening appeared in Becky's day care center, Max advised Liz to apply. (He and Liz were old, dear friends.) She did. Was turned down. Becky refused to recommend her.

"Holy smoke," Max yelled, "she's your good friend, she wants a job. How come you refuse her?"

"What's her being a friend have to do with it? The purpose of a day care center is to give intelligent care to children whose parents have to work. They do not need someone to come in to woo them with a love so effusive that they become awed spectators to Miss Universe doing her jazz act for applause. Liz is fun to go to a gallery with, to have entertain your guests at a dinner party, even to see a movie with—she's pretty damned good at giving it a very sharp critique, though she always seems to miss the fun in great comedies, with those she feels ill at ease because they might very well be poking fun at *her*. But she's no damned good for children. Look at her own." A low blow.

"You're just jealous."

"Hardly, Max. Even though you can't keep your eyes, even the glass one, from following every move of her ass."

"Forget it."

"It is forgotten, Max." It wasn't, because Rebecca knew Max had had a go with Liz, as what male friend hadn't?

It had taken Max some time, but he finally learned to appreciate Becky's ability to distinguish the genuine article from paste.

Friends, family, siblings across the land, and she had six of them, her mother Ruth in the old-age home in Springfield, Massachusetts, Max, her children, all believed they knew Becky. Miss Perfect. It was obvious, wasn't it, that she was what she appeared to be on the surface? After all, wasn't she always up front, as the kids said? She was the Golden Lady, the Great Pacifier, the Victorian Lady, all of which infuriated Becky. Though she didn't remain angry or infuriated very long, which was one of her problems. In one of Edith Hamilton's books she read about a Greek general who came upon a leveled, dead and forgotten city state. As he browsed about the rubble in what once must have been the *agora*, he was stopped by a wall bearing the inscription: *They forgot how to be angry.* It was signed by the conquering commander.

So Rebecca tried to sustain her anger when she thought it was deserved, but somehow nearly always failed. It seemed so silly and irrational, as exemplified by that ridiculous business with young Tucciano, one of Eli's close friends and former football teammates, who stopped to stare at her with his dark passionate eyes (how like Dominic's) everytime they crossed paths in town. At first Becky became angry with him, then realized it was ludicrous and laughed. The poor kid had become obsessed since that time, while working for his father installing combination storms and screens, he climbed the ladder and surprised Rebecca—and himself—in the bathroom, naked, sitting on the pot of all things. Only quick reflexes saved him from falling and breaking his foolish young neck and her from flooding the tile floor. Then he appeared at the side window of the day care center, his intense eyes drilling into her back until she could actually feel them. She really let him have it then. Unbowed, unashamed, he strode away. Yet a few days later, he parked his black Thunderbird in front of the house a few hours before she was to leave for work. She pretended to take no notice of it, it was too silly. Then he did it the next morning, and the next. She was going to tell Max about it, but decided not to, he would probably break the boy's neck. And besides, it was amusing, *The Roman Spring of Mrs. Miller*. Young Tucciano was obsessed, one day soon he would realize she was a fifty-year-old woman, think better of it and go away. Why get angry about it?

Yes, Rebecca insisted on peace, seemed always to run from a fight, would rather laugh than cry. But Eli, not yet satisfied that he had captured the truth of his mother on canvas, decided to have another go at it. A true artist, he believed, must know everything there is to know about his subject, even if to gain that knowledge he must be deceitful, must steal, do almost anything, be as irrational as a true believer, a fundamentalist in religion or politics, use anything at all, even terror, to gain his objective. Or so Eli had understood, perhaps misunderstood, when his art professor, Raphael Eliason—a happy confluence of names—had declaimed in class that to become a great artist one must be obsessed with the subject of one's canvas, even if it is an apple. One must love that apple, caress that apple, even fornicate with that apple. Of course, Eli did not intend to fornicate with his mother, even he knew that was an evil beyond all other evils, and after all the professor had only been speaking metaphorically. Unforgivable as it was, Eli decided that he must read his mother's private journals kept, since she was fifteen years old, because an admired high school English teacher had told her if she was some day to become a writer, it would be wise to begin to keep a commonplace book and a diary. His mother kept these journals in the antique chestnut secretary in his parents' bedroom.

Choosing the day and time carefully, since he knew the family's whereabouts almost to the minute—Mom would be at work, Pop in New York at the International's office preparing for his trip to North Carolina, Nina was up at the lake staying with the Dubins before returning home to leave for prep school, and Peter down in the Village working on Zorah's boutique—Eli took the early afternoon train to Highview and then a cab to the house. So impatient was he to learn his mother's secrets, he didn't even notice the familiar sleek T-bird parked in front of the house. He ran up the porch steps, and as he passed the window to the living room, the glint of his mother's red-gold hair through the translucent curtains captured his attention. He stopped at the window to peek. Immediately wished he were blind. Wanted to turn and run, couldn't. Lot's wife . . . a pillar of salt. His lips quivered, became tight from sudden loss of blood. His heart drummed mercilessly. Dizziness, nausea like an overwhelming seasickness overcame him. In slow motion he pulled himself away from the window. Tears at the rims of his eyes, weak-kneed, with great caution he retraced his steps down the porch stairs, stared now at the highly waxed black Thunderbird with recognition, then sick to his stomach, ashen-faced, Eli began to run down the block.

He just ran and ran.

Rebecca knitted Max's sweater while sitting on the porch, the fragmented September sun's rays warming her back. One part of her mind was on the timer in the kitchen, set for eleven when she wanted to phone her mother, another part on Shep Nielson about whom she'd begun to think of more often lately. Guilt, guilt, once you've earned it, it becomes a more intimate part of you than your own flesh and bones. Now she had a new guilt to add to the others. At last, though, she'd satisfied her curiosity about what it was everyone was always talking, even bragging, about. Big deal! She couldn't help smiling to herself. Anything Liz Morrison can do, I can do better. Phoney friend. It was the sort of guilt that deserved only one mea culpa. The mere remembrance of what had happened thirty-five years ago in Shep's studio still caused her more pain and guilt than this little affair deserved. One afternoon, as Shep was positioning her on the chair and she was looking into his eyes—her own eyes, she was certain, overflowing with love—he began to breathe quickly and awkwardly ran the palm of his hand over her already bountifully filled blouse, abruptly pulled back, turned, and went stiffly to stand at his easel. He stood with his back towards her for a few moments, then began painting. Unusual for him, he remained silent the rest of the afternoon. Already fifteen and yet still so innocent that to her it had been no more than if he had touched her arm. Not quite. She knew it was more than that, but hardly. More than hardly. Admit it, Rebecca. You'd won a victory over Mama, enough of a victory to make you blush with shame, and elation, as you walked home. Shep finished the painting after two or three more sittings, resuming as before his easy conversations with her, and that was the end of it. Shortly thereafter he moved into the house. A lovely man, his behavior was never anything but punctiliously correct towards her and her sisters, and to Mama he was marvelous, gave her great happiness until he became ill and died at an early age. Dear man. The painting was in Mimi's attic with the rest of Mama's stuff, an amateurish work, color and craftsmanship poor—he had, alas, not been a very good painter.

The timer buzzed, and as she dialed the kitchen phone,

she couldn't help murmur to herself, "Forgive me, Mama, if I caused you pain. You knew, didn't you, you knew?"

"Hello, hello."

"Hello, Ma."

"Polly?"

"No, Ma, this is Becky. How are you?"

"Oh . . . well."

"Oh well what?"

"I'm all right, I guess."

"Is there anything wrong?"

"I'm fine. It just hurts. How's Max, the children?"

"As far as I know they are all well. I'll probably come up to see you next week. Is there anything you want?"

"What do I want?"

Like me, Rebecca thought, she wants everything. "Polly comes several times a week. So does Emanuel. Sophie writes you long letters a couple times a month, Mimi, too. I come frequently to visit, call you almost every other day . . ."

Mama laughed. "I'm greedy. Do you have to remind me?"

Now Becky laughed, too. She was also greedy. "Are you walking yet?"

"What do I need to walk for, I've got the deaf one to push me around. He loves to push." Mama laughed again.

"Push him back, Ma."

"I wish I could, what do you think?" Now they both laughed.

"Have you heard from Nina, Eli?"

"They write very often—they're good grandchildren, better than my own sons."

"You haven't heard from Jack then?"

"He means well, he's too busy, poor man." Where her mother always could forgive Jack, she could never forgive the others. "Your Nina tells me everything—doesn't leave out a thing—tells me things I don't even want to know. How could you let her go off to private school at her age. Not yet sixteen—a baby. I'm surprised Max let her go."

"She wanted to go. She got a scholarship. We let her go. Don't worry about her—though I must say I'm sorry now myself, but for me, not for her. You know, Ma, you were barely older than her when you left your parents and came to a strange land, perhaps never to see your mother and father again. Remember?"

"Well, things were different then. We became grownups at ten, not forty like today."

Rebecca wanted to say, "Not forty, not even fifty," but said instead, "Don't worry about—"

"Everyone says don't worry. I don't worry, the pain in my hip is too much. I can't sleep, can't walk. I'm finished, Beckeleh."

"The doctor said if you'd try to walk it would heal faster. Try it and see."

"Here comes Harry, such a nice man."

Rebecca giggled. "There's plenty of life in you still, Ma."

"You're keeping my apartment, paying the rent?"

"Of course," Rebecca lied, and knew her mother was aware she was lying. "By the way, do you mind if I take Shep's portrait of me? I'd like to have it."

Without even a breath's hesitation, Mama answered, "But of course you can take it, it's yours."

Thank God, Mama had forgiven her at last. "Okay, Mom, see you next week I hope."

"Bring me a fresh chalah and a quarter pound of Philadelphia cream cheese. The food here is lousy. Give Max my regards."

"He sends his."

"Becky?"

"Yes?"

"Why do you sound so sad?"

"Me?"

"I am not deaf yet, I can hear very well. Is there something wrong between you and Max?"

"No!"

"I'm sorry, I shouldn't interfere in your life."

"You can interfere all you goddamn please, you're my mother."

"This isn't like you, what's wrong?"

"I'm sorry, Ma. I don't have to tell you, you know yourself, and know it very well, when you have children, a husband, a life to live yourself, there's always something, always something . . ."

Her mother sighed. "Yes, yes, I know. And it's time you knew, my child, not even the Devil can stop the clock from ticking."

They were both silent for a moment.

"Be well, Becky."

"You, too, Ma."

When Rebecca picked up her knitting again, she had tears in her eyes. Mothers with their antennae! Well, she was a mother, too! The clock never stops ticking. . . . There was the purr of a motor in front of the house, and she hurried down the porch steps to catch him before he opened the car door. She then leaned against it so he couldn't get out. His dark brown eyes were still very intense, yet she could see the obsession was gone, slaked, satisfied. Good.

"No more," she said firmly. "It was very nice. You will be a gentleman, I'm sure, and not say anything."

"Of course," he said. "You're a great lady."

"Thanks."

He smiled, nodded, threw the stick into first and slid away from the curb.

The circle closes . . . round and round. . . . Strange.

While having a spot of lunch, Becky heard the postman at the box. She hurried out to the porch. Nothing from Peter, the little stinker, but another fat letter from Nina. Rebecca smiled.

NINA-5

Dear Mom and Dad,

I know this letter is coming soon after the last one, but
I'm really just dying to tell you about Richard so that I'm
writing it this late at night when I should be sleeping—
dying to tell you, Dad, because he's so crazy he'd make
you flip, and you, Mom, because he'd be great material
for your journal, and you, parents, because he is the new
man in my life. (I can hear Dad saying, "Jeezu, waddashe-
need another one for, she eats 'em like peanuts." Well—
don't worry, this relationship is not very serious—in fact
it's not at all in existence at the moment.) He's the crush I
thought it would take months to know, but you know
me, spoiled rotten, wants something—gets something.
No, seriously, I met him through Louise and it's just that
he and I have been talking a lot lately. Shall I start with
the character Richard, or the messed-up Richard? I think
the former. He's a bit like Pete. He's got an incredibly
good imagination and incredibly bad luck. This explains
the luck, not the imagination: a few weeks ago he came
up to visit Carol the bragger—he's friends with her, too—
at about 3:00 A.M. and as he was leaving he nearly ran into
Mr. Leonard, the housefather. So, somehow, he thinks
he's on the first floor (ground) when he's really on the second, and he runs into what he thinks is Louise's room,
jumps on the bed, and attempts to scramble over it and
out the window. Joanie, in the meantime, hit with a person jumping on her bed, and with thoughts of (1) rape or
(2) a desperate girl trying to commit suicide out *her* win-

dow for some reason, screams bloody murder. Richard, scared out of his wits, falls off the bed—luckily on the room side and not out the window, and then jumps into the closet. Joanie by this time realizes what's going on, and doesn't say a word. *But* (this is true I swear), meantime Richard finds that when he scrambles into the closet he bumps into another person already there—now it's his turn to scream. The other person turns out to be a friend of Richard's who had been visiting a girl living next door to Joanie, and who, having heard Mr. Leonard walking the halls, had snuck into Joanie's closet seconds before Richard's arrival. Well, Mr. Leonard, not being deaf to *two* screams, enters the room and the boys finally decide to be courageous and come out of "hiding." They both got three-day stayovers and were put on probation.

Is that a hilarious story or what? Richard told it lots better (with help from Bob, the other body in the closet) and had me laughing for twenty minutes. By the way, all this took place directly across the hall from me and I slept through the whole thing.

He's told me other stories but that was one of the best. He's so funny. He has these facial expressions which are so incredible they never fail to make me break up. One of them is closing his eyes, blowing his face up so hard his nose gets lost, and then scrunching his mouth in so that it looks like an asshole in a fat red behind. I almost burst when he did it for me, and actually had to run to the bathroom before I did it in my pants.

I s'pose you must hear the bad, too. Now, you mustn't worry about what I'm getting myself into because there's no point to that—nothing will rub off onto me—if anything I'll become stronger in what I am, and also I am keeping myself uninvolved because it seems, Daddy, I am eating 'em like peanuts and I don't wanna mess myself up making out with a different boy every week. Okay?

Richard is definitely fouled up. He's one of those unfortunate people who get caught up in a circle. He is the "typical" rebellious son of an affluent businessman. He's messed up on drugs—not addictive ones—he snorts. Great, huh? Well, he's only done it three times in two months, so I guess that should make me a little happy. I mean he's not wasted all the time by any means, and since he's met me he's stopped because I won't talk to him when he's high because it bothers me, and then also he's got zero self-discipline it seems to me, and very few values. I mean schoolwise. Talking to him it's obvious he's got a good brain—a very good one, but he doesn't "like" to work. His parents are constantly on his back, which does *nothing*.

I guess, Mom & Dad, what I feel like doing with Richard is just holding him close to me, cuddling him, you know. I don't mean actually *sleep* with him except maybe if he's on top of the blanket and I'm under it. I just feel so *sorry* for him.

So that's this week's story of Poor Richard. Don't worry—I can handle it.

I love you both!

Nina xxxxxxxxxx

THE DEVIL WITH IT

"Hiya, Beck."

"Darling!"

"Jesus, it sounds good to hear your voice."

"It's only been a couple of—"

"You keeping busy?"

"Busy enough. I—"

"I—"

"Let me say it first for a change."

Max laughed. "Go ahead, I'm all ears."

"I want you lying on top of me."

"Just close your eyes and think of it."

"No, we mustn't start what we can't finish."

"Don't be a puritan, honey, you can finish anything we start."

"I'd rather wait. I'm old-fashioned."

"Quit boasting."

"I'm sorry."

"Maybe I can lock these lunkheads in the meeting room over the weekend, sneak out, grab a plane, be in the house in two, three hours, we can wreck the bed—inside out, right side up, upside down, any old way—and be back here before morning. Boy, that last time—hey! there it is."

"What, Max?"

"Look at the damn thing!"

"Perhaps what we needed was a vacation from each other."

"Maybe."

"What's wrong, Max, you suddenly sound down."

"It is. When you said that, you were saying it hasn't been up to snuff lately."

"For goodness sake, Max, it's been wonderful, who cares about—"

"Sorry. Women don't have the same worries men do about these things. Forget it. Have you heard from Pete?"

"Nothing. Another letter from Nina, though. Strangely enough, I haven't heard from Eli for weeks, and he's never home when I phone."

"Maybe he's gone off with Kathy Dubin. As for Pete, he'll be all right—he's not easily conned. I wrote Nina a letter tonight. Boy, she doesn't leave out a detail, does she? I wish Pete told us everything like she does."

"What does it look like down there?"

"It's still up, Beck."

Rebecca laughed, and it sounded like music. "Save it for me," she said through the laugh.

"Don't worry, I'm no fool."

"How long does it look like you'll have to be in the South?"

"We might be able to wrap up a contract faster than I first thought. Will know in another day or two. Tell you the truth, I'm getting tired of this work. I already told Sid Dubin that I want to stay in New York."

"That would be awfully nice. By the way, how's your movie coming along?"

"I know the whole movie, honey, but I don't know the ending yet. Will I end up in an old-age home like your mother?"

"No, Max, we won't."

"We won't, then why is she there when we have a big fucking house in which she can rattle around?"

"She lived with us a long time, and now she can't be alone in her own apartment or with us. I like to get out of the house, I enjoy my work, and we can't afford a full-time nurse. That's why. Why do you always try to make me feel guilty about her?"

"All right, all right. I'm sorry. I know the story. Can't one of your brothers or sisters take her in?"

"Same story, Max. In the old days women stayed at home, but nowadays women go to work, have lives to live outside the home. So the old people go to old-age homes."

"So will we, kiddo, so will we. Unless we're lucky enough to die first."

"It's not that bad there."

"Sitting with all those old crocks—"

"But, Max, she's old, too."

"Okay. Maybe some day when all the other million problems are settled, we'll find a solution for this one."

Becky laughed. "Max Miller, the eternal optimist, thinks all the million problems are going to be solved. There will always be a million problems to solve—always. Get that into your thick skull, Max Miller."

"Yeah, I get it. But how can you live without believing you can cure every disease?"

"By living in reality, not in a movie. In a movie, you can bring everything to a nice neat conclusion, but in life you can't. You just can't control everything, Max."

"Suppose so. . . . Say, Becky, what's with you? You've talked more tonight than in a month of Sundays?"

"Listen, Max, never look a gift horse in the behind—it might very well fart."

Max laughed with a roar, and then Becky joined him.

"It was good talking to you, Max."

"You don't think of cheating, do you?"

"With whom? The milkman? I gave him up as soon as Nina went off."

"Sometimes I start worrying that I'm getting too old for you, just when you're hitting your prime. You could use a good young—"

"Stop it, you mean more to me than a dozen young cocks possibly could. If you can sneak home, I'll be waiting for you showered and perfumed."

"Goodnight, Beck."

"You know what Mama said to me on the phone—not

even the Devil can stop the clock from ticking. So don't you go chasing after some young chick either."

Max laughed, and then they kissed each other good-bye over the phone . . .

Becky, who'd been reading in bed when Max called, turned off the light and relaxed under the cotton blanket. She still heard Max's laugh in her ears and couldn't repress a smile. If he didn't watch out, she'd soon be talking him under the table. Now she laughed, turned on her side, closed her eyes, and was soon fast asleep.

Not Max. He lay in the darkness in his hotel bed, his eye closed, but the fake one a flickering silver screen inside his head . . .

CLOSE SHOT: Rebecca, showered and perfumed, is lying naked on the large double bed in the Miller bedroom. A shaded bed lamp reveals her ample body, the rest of the room is in semi-darkness. The large brown eyes in her bony elegant face are mere slits, her lips, moist and swollen, are partially open; her soft breasts recline under her shoulders, the aureoles puckered and swollen, too; her soft belly rises and falls. She has a thick red muff; her hips are broad, narrowing to still shapely thighs and legs. Her knees are slightly open . . .

She smiles and raises her soft white arms as from the semi-darkness Max Miller nakedly approaches the bed. He is a brawny man, in the shadows the gray hair on his head like curled horns. His bad eye is closed, his good eye wide open and glaring maniacally; his legs taper down to hooves, and behind him a tail swishes. He stands ajut . . . FADE OUT.

Max sleeps.
The Devil grins.
The clock ticks.

Temple Israel

Minneapolis, Minnesota

IN HONOR OF THE BAR MITZVAH OF
JONATHAN LIEBERMAN
FROM
MERLE SEGAL & FAMILY